H.E.A.V.E.N.

AUGUST 11 - 28, 2073

Nan Becklean

2nd Edition

Originally published by Booklocker

This edition published 2013 by Nan Becklean Tobin

Copyright © 2009 Nan Becklean

The Author asserts the moral right to be identified as the author of this work

A CIP catalogue record for this book is available from the British Library.

ISBN: 978-0-9884868-2-9

nanbooks.com

CONTENTS

For Austin,
my children and grandchildren:
Jen, Rich, Liz, Bo, Jordan, Dylan, Nicholas, Hallie,
Nikita and Natalie

Characters in order of appearance

Sarah Rally, *resident of H.E.A.V.E.N.*
Jeff Rally, *Sarah's husband*
Ben, *robot extraordinaire, Pine Haven's number one guard*
Lionel Questar, *Senator and Living Treasure*
Babe, *Sarah's dog*
Melody Graves, *singer/composer and Angelic*
Roy Desroy, *robotician at Pine Haven*
Tessa Posnoff, *eroticist at Pine Haven*
Wilbur, *Roy's tiny robot*
Huxley Soong, *lead guitarist of The CrossOvers in Swyannah*
Harriet Soong, *Huxley's mother, new resident of H.E.A.V.E.N.*
Investigator Krantz, *of Swyannah's police force*
Zack Dakota, *pilot*
Annemarie Posnoff, *Tessa's sister*
Clarissa, *Sarah and Jeff's daughter*
Tom, *Pine Haven life guard*
Harry Plato, *Pine Haven Head of Maintenance*
Mrs. Burch, *Roy's mother*
Grot, *one of the six lesser robots guarding Pine Haven*

Referenced characters

Granny, Sarah's beloved, deceased grandmother
Barkley, *Sarah and Jeff's son*
Conway Questar, *Lionel's deceased father*
Ginger, *Lionel's beloved deceased dog*
Huck Soong, *Huxley's famous deceased father*
Louella, Olivia and Pamela, *Lionel's deceased wives*
Aunt Edna, *Huxley's deceased clairvoyant aunt*
Bob Questar and Billy Questar, *Lionel's twin sons*

Places

Pine Haven, *one of H.E.A.V.E.N.'s many island locations*
Swyannah, *southern city across the bay from Pine Haven*
Darby, *Hometown of Roy and Mrs. Burch*
The StrataDrome
The coast of Maine

FRIDAY, AUGUST 11, 2073

Only two weeks and a day till her ninety-fifth birthday. Sarah sighed and scrutinized the calendar on her omniplus.

"It seems I've lived forever," she murmured. "Long enough anyway." But now with death certain in seventeen days thanks to her contract with the State, she had changed her mind. She wanted to hit one hundred or more—yes, live as long as she could. Why not?

The whole thing, after all, had been Jeff's idea, his fault. She could see him, still a hunk at eighty-four, striding onto the porch one summer afternoon in 2060 wearing his best salesman smile.

"Sarah," he said in the deep voice he used for important matters. "We need to talk."

That meant it would be about doing something she wouldn't want to do and this time she hadn't seen it coming. They both had watched and made fun of the government's propaganda ads and Sarah never thought it would become an issue. After all, HEAVEN wasn't mandatory.

But now Jeff said it was necessary.

"Don't you realize my life-expectancy is one-hundred twenty and yours is one-hundred twenty-five?" he asked. "Is that crazy or what?" He opened his eyes wide and stared into hers. "Only Living Treasures can afford to hang around that long!"

"Oh," Sarah said. "I thought we had enough to get by."

"Get by? Maybe so—but I don't want to pinch pennies for the rest of my life and I don't think you do either," Jeff said. "Also, who knows what will happen to the cost of living? It could skyrocket."

"I guess," Sarah said.

"It's happened before. Remember two-thousand thirty-six."

"You're right."

"Wouldn't it be great to have a permanent non-stop vacation?"

"I like our life as it is," Sarah said.

"Think about what a terrific break it will be for *you*. No more heating the qwikchow—no household chores, no bills to pay—no more worries of any kind for either of us. And," he added, "who wants to live past ninety-five anyway? Isn't it quality of life, not quantity?"

And on and on—all that hoop-de-do he was so good at when he sold insurance. What he didn't say was that he didn't want his hard-earned money to go to the State. Never mind principle—it was a matter of principal. Actually, it was both.

Plus he was disgusted with his Boomer parents who had cashed out, spent everything, and then come to live with him and Sarah until their deaths at one hundred and eight and nine, which they greeted with wailing, tears and shouts of "I'm not ready," and "It isn't fair."

Later, Jeff discovered that his parents were typical of their generation—living longer than expected and wanting to live even longer. Medicine, healthy habits and science kept seventy-five percent of them, born in the late 1940s, alive and jogging past one hundred. The country nearly went broke paying Social Security benefits alone.

Something had to be done. The President and both sides of the aisle unified. They changed the tax code so the rich and the corporations were paying taxes without loopholes; the estate tax was reinstated; Social Security and Medicare contributions were increased to a combined eighteen-percent—wage earners paid into both funds, no matter how high their incomes; the age for retirement was upped to seventy-five; and people became seniors and eligible for Social Security and Medicare at eighty.

None of it was enough.

Actuaries eventually determined that it would only be enough if people stopped living so long.

And so the states, after much wrangling, rallied together and passed the Forty-first Amendment, the Homeland Equitable Alliance for a Victimless Economy and Nation, or HEAVEN. That was in 2056.

HEAVEN offered a luxurious coda to life for people who agreed to a date-certain for extinction. The outcry against the proposed solution was quashed by a government advertising blitz presenting the specter of vigorous old people living in luxury in contrast to overworked, nearly starving young couples unable to care for themselves or their children because so much of their income went to caring for the elderly.

This was followed by a campaign to attract registrations by citizens even if it would be years until they were eligible.

When you choose HEAVEN, the ad's dancing letters announced, *your last years will be spent in a spectacular dreamland designed for your comfort and delight at no charge*!

"I can't wait!" Pitt Leonardo, a handsome, graying actor said, and flashed his splendid teeth.

A famous journalist, Herbert Frankenfall, appeared at his side and prepared to dive into a blue-waved sea.

"Come on, folks. What's there to think about? Just say yes."

"Do it for us," two solemn-faced pre-schoolers pleaded.

The word FREE flew from side to side within the wall-to-wall. It swooped over the heads of lithe older people playing golf on wide fairways or tennis on shaded courts, or swimming in lucent lakes or running on paths flanked by green fields full of blue Chinese forget-me-nots and flame-red poppies.

Mona Livingwell, a celebrity expert on lifestyles said, "You will be guaranteed gourmet organic meals whenever you prefer them to flavored meal pills. In addition you will receive health care, prescriptions, all operations, corrective facial and bodily surgery, even organ and hair transplants."

"A biannual workup will assess your mineral, vitamin, hormonal, electrolyte and fiber needs to create a custom add-on potion to your diet," Alice Greenbody, a famous nutritionist promised.

A former Treasury secretary, Midas Buckmeister, explained, "Best of all, you will be able to bequeath all of your assets to anyone without incurring federal or state tax."

Euge (Eugene) Head, a recently retired news commentator said, "For these privileges, all you need to do is sign an agreement that will allow you to depart this life in a state of ecstasy at age ninety or, if you prefer, earlier."

By the time Jeff and Sarah joined the HEAVEN program, the retirement and entrance age had been moved up to eighty-five and Departure from HEAVEN, ninety-five.

They drove to the agency to sign the necessary papers.

"Here's to Golden Years Limited," Jeff said raising an imaginary glass.

"That's not funny, Jeff. This is serious and it's scary," Sarah said. "I want to think about it some more."

"Come on! We've hashed it out over and over. A decade of guaranteed bliss awaits us. That's a long time."

"Ha," Sarah said. "The last ten years whipped by in about six months."

"Don't exaggerate. Think about how nice it will be for Clarissa and Barkley. They'll inherit everything as soon as we're in HEAVEN."

"Is this all about them?"

"No way. I just don't want them waiting for us to die or worse—wishing we would. Remember how it was with my parents. We could hardly wait for them to go. This way it's a done deal."

"Like a prepaid whole life insurance policy?"

"Sarah, Sarah," Jeff chided. "The point is—we'll never be a burden."

Neither took in the reality of the program until Jeff died in perfect health to live up to its dictum when, as promised, he was in a state of ecstasy before and at the time of death. He was dressed for a swim, lying on a chaise when he died, face aglow, his hand hot in Sarah's. She felt it cool, saw him wax pale yellow, heard his last laugh shoot through the sunlit air over the sand and out to sea.

Jeff was scheduled to precede her by two years, three months and twelve days, giving her the benefit of more time in HEAVEN, a concession by the State to married couples close in age who had the foresight to petition for the privilege. She could have elected to go with him, but their children voted no, so she waited and continued to experience the extraordinary life the citizens provided her, which, if they lived long enough and so chose, they would eventually enjoy themselves.

Recently, scenes appeared and stayed in a corner of her head, unbidden, or she'd smell a scent from long ago and be back somewhere, under the funny old scrub tree outside her grandma's house with a stick she'd peeled and sharpened to dig in the dark tight earth. Or with her tiny black and white terrier licking her face as she carried her to the corner store for a bag of corn candy; or rocking with her children on her lap, reading a story, breathing in their just-bathed, baby scent.

Often, time laid itself out as flat as a quilt and she saw things as if they were happening simultaneously. Maybe they were, or maybe it was the effect of the Exaltation pill she took daily, now that her Celebration and Departure were imminent.

She'd passed through life like a skiff through water, a shallow wake, then no trace. True, she'd been recognized as a competent designer of cy-spaces created in her home office while the children were growing up, and she'd served on various boards to improve whatever needed improving, build whatever needed building—but not one thing was worth recording or mentioning in an obituary. She'd never considered it before, but now her insignificance bothered her and it was way too late to do anything about it—or was it? Maybe she could do something spectacular—something deserving of wall-to-wall news and a headline in the two extant newspapers, one per coast.

Maybe she could jump off a floating way station using an old-fashioned parachute. That would definitely be newsworthy given her age and status and merit a huge spread in celebrity and calamity magazines, more popular, crude, outrageous and inaccurate than ever.

Or she could escape. Had anyone ever done that? Outwitted the robots, the Prolocutor and pulled a fast one on the State? Doubtful. But it was worth a try.

Since coming to HEAVEN, her head had been clear of its static—the to-do lists, the anxious conversations with herself about whether or not she'd said or done the right thing and she realized no one had ever given a good goddamn what she said or did. Not when she gave birth to two children, not when she kept them fed, clean, well-spoken, mannerly and wrapped in a love she liked to think was unconditional.

Not when she baked cakes and pies from scratch, or made quilts by hand and hung them in craft shows, or sewed and lined her curtains, or spent every Tuesday at the Ladies Auxiliary checking in clothes and attaching missing buttons.

And here she was, living in a house without curtains, wearing clothes without buttons. Her usual choice was a silky jumpsuit, often with an aqua motif, the predictable match of her eyes. She was predictable, had always been predictable. She saw her younger self with a kind of dismay. She remembered that it used to be important to find someone who understood her. Whatever did that mean? What was there to understand about anyone?

She must have bored many people with her life story, and now was in awe of their ancient patience with her. *How fascinated we all are with ourselves,* she thought, *but not with anyone else, not really except as a link back to number-one.*

Now lust was gone. She'd never had more than two: sex and acceptance—not that they went together—and not that she knew it at the time. What she knew then was that it was important what everyone, including the dogs and the cat, thought of her and whether or not everyone was happy. It was hard to tell. If anyone wasn't, or if anything went wrong, it was obviously her fault. Why was she like that? It didn't matter; she just was.

Her first husband had pursued her relentlessly but once married, was seldom interested in sex. Not, that is, until he found out she'd had an affair. The crazy thing was she'd had the affair because he had rejected her so often she could no longer stand for him to touch her unless she had too much to drink. And although she continued to drink too much and thus permitted his more frequent post-affair marital demands, they divorced. Three years later, she married Jeff.

Jeff, on the other hand, was interested in sex—very interested. Perhaps too interested if there were such a thing, and there clearly was because one woman wasn't enough. But she didn't know that until their children were in school and she'd restarted the business that had introduced her to Jeff to begin with. He'd been first a client, then a lover, then a husband.

She had thought it best to ignore his philandering partly—she told herself—for the sake of the children and partly—she told herself—because it was better to be married to a man of immoderate warmth than a man of uncommon coolness—as if all men were one or the other—but mostly because she adored his sea-scent, his rough hair, his quirky brain.

The first time he cheated—if it was the first time— there'd been hell to pay. She'd left him for two weeks and, after her return, didn't speak to him for months. Much later when he was eighty, he agreed to go with her to a *Take Your Marriage to the Next Level* weekend and promised to be faithful forever. It wasn't much of a sacrifice—by then forever didn't seem so far off, nor was he so hot to trot—but at least it made their final years together happier—at least for her.

She was still in love with Jeff and had believed it would be a relief when her time to Depart arrived—she knew absolutely she would see him again. Then some long dormant resentment surfaced and she changed her mind.

"I'm not ready to die," she told her dog. "And I'm mad at Jeff."

Sarah heard a familiar murmur. She looked up. Ben, robot extraordinaire, and first among six other robot crocodiles approached. He was her favorite. Next to her dog, Babe, she loved him best.

"The perfect end to a perfect day," Ben declared to each person or open door he cruised by in his area of responsibility, one-seventh of Pine Haven Island. "Temperature seventy-seven degrees, skies clear, ocean calm. Breeze from the south, two miles an hour."

He paused at Sarah's terrace.

"What time is it, Ben?" she asked, smiling.

"Five-twenty. Lionel's on his way."

Sarah nodded. "You know everything," she said.

Just then, over the dunes, she saw Lionel coming toward her house, kicking the sand, as usual, like a kid. He was going to adopt Babe.

Lionel's father, Conway Questar, had been right. Lionel *was* one lucky son of a bitch, which was what Conway always said about people he liked and envied. Even so, he would have been amazed to see Lionel elected to the House, then the Senate several times, or twice chosen as his party's nominee for president.

But Conway wasn't around because of a windsurfing accident that had drowned him off the Virginia shore during a Fourth of July beach party in 2012. He had expected a girl visiting from California to fall for his big chest and skilled maneuvering, as others had in the past, but she had been eating crab and looking in the other direction the entire time.

The fourth time Conway turned to squint her way, the afternoon sun shot a ray into his right eye. He lost his balance, fell off, hit his head on the board, went under and didn't come up until the next morning when he rolled into shore.

"I was only in my thirties at the time, a late bloomer just finishing college," Lionel told reporters when asked how he got started in politics. "I was blessed," he liked to say, meaning he had inherited his father's large, white teeth, broad smile, confident manner and thick, dark-blond hair, along with a big chunk of his portfolio.

He was most grateful for the latter, though each personal attribute had come in handy over the years, and many believed his hair had got him elected when his stand on domestic, foreign and beyond-Earth matters proved to be indistinguishable from that of his less hirsute adversaries in the Repucratic and Demoblican Parties. Both advocated Land Sacrifice in the wake of global warming but differed on which land was expendable and which should be raised in place or protected by dikes.

They also differed on how many children a couple should be allowed to produce in the face of an exacerbating population blowout. Demoblicans believed one was enough while the Repucratics were in favor of one and a half, which meant states would have to negotiate with its citizens to achieve the desirable average. Credits would be given to each state for couples that opted to remain childless. A vote for an amendment to put either proposal into the constitution had not yet passed and, for the time being, people of childbearing age remained on the honor system to have a maximum of two.

It also may have been his hair that got him chosen as a Living Treasure. Lionel's mane was even more magnificent when it turned a luminous gray. And name recognition helped. By age eighty-five, Lionel had been a senator for forty-two years and as pilot of his little silver duoplane, the unforgettable symbol of the ethic, 'Get up and fly.'

After closing up his two homes—an antique ski-chalet in Sony Valley, a historic Greek Revival in Scarlettesville—Lionel spent most of his time at Pine Haven's HEAVEN off the coast of Georgia, where there was plenty to do if he so chose and the food was excellent; he preferred the practice of eating to swallowing meal pills and potions. He was content there until his companion of twenty-five years died. He couldn't sleep without Ginger's warm body pressed against him. When he saw Sarah's ad in *The Nirvana Dispatch* for her fifteen-year-old mixed breed he got in touch at once.

"Don't like purebreds," Lionel had grumbled over the omniplus. "Want a mutt, and they're hard to find. Nothing but purebreds around these days."

"You'll like Babe," Sarah had replied, her arms around the little black and white dog. "No one knows what she is."

"She?"

"Yes." *Hadn't he heard her the first time?*

"Well, damn. Ginger was a he."

"Oh well, never mind then," Sarah said.

"No, no, I'll be right over. Don't show her to anyone else."

That started the late-afternoon routine of Lionel stopping by to play with Babe. After the first two visits,

Babe bounded out the door when she saw him. Lionel always had a biscuit and a stick or a ball. "Let's go, girl," he would say.

Then they would play for half an hour. Lionel wanted to take the dog away with him every time but, as Sarah pointed out a few weeks later when she felt more at ease with her new friend, she needed to keep Babe around for comfort until the very end.

"What do you mean the end?" Lionel had long ago read and forgotten the by-laws of HEAVEN.

"My God, Lionel, don't you get it? My Departure is scheduled for August twenty-eighth, two weeks from this coming Monday. That's why I need a home for my darling dog."

Babe sat on her lap, staring at Lionel.

"But you're so smashing," Lionel said.

"Thanks for that, but I'm almost ninety-five." She crossed her toned legs and smiled.

"I'm nearly a hundred," Lionel said. He smiled back.

"We all look good, Lionel, thanks to the procedures." And who cared? She was about to be history, smashing or not.

"Damn." Lionel groaned, a sorrowful crease forming either side of his mouth.

"What's the matter?" Sarah asked.

"I like you." He touched Sarah on her slim, youthful hand. "You'll be missed."

"Thank you, Lionel. That's very sweet. I like you, too. But unless I think of a way out, it looks as if I'll have to keep my bargain with the State, although I'd give anything not to. It's not that I'm afraid to die. I just don't want to."

Lionel abruptly realized he would have Departed long ago if he weren't a Living Treasure—he was five years past HEAVEN's deadline, and felt good enough to last another ten. "Understandable," he said.

"And lately, I've started to look back at my life—my marriage in particular—and now I'm angry with Jeff. I mean why did I put up with his cheating all those years? I must've been out of my mind." Sarah breathed in deeply. "Sorry," she said. "Maybe I'll just ask Melody to give me an extra Exaltation pill."

"Hmm. I'd like to try one of those," Lionel mused.

Sarah wasn't listening. "I was fine when Jeff was alive. There wasn't much time to think. We were busy doing stuff all the time. We jogged on the beach every morning with Babe. Swam, surfed, played gin, double solitaire and backgammon, had omniskin surgeries and parts replacements, inside and out. Lifted weights in the Space Station replica. I still do that every other day."

She paused. "We went to the Sex Center twice a week. Had sex. Did puzzles, played expograms, stood on our heads, meditated, attained partial enlightenment. Sometimes we climbed the Monument to the Past. Best of all, we raced our glitterplanes against other couples."

"No kidding," Lionel said,

"We were champions," said Sarah.

"I love to fly," Lionel said.

"I know. Do you still have that silver duoplane?"

"Of course. I enter antique plane shows."

"Do you fly it?"

"That's what I'm saying. Sometimes we win, Ginger and I." Lionel stopped, touched his forehead. "Damn, I forgot."

"I'm sorry," Sarah said.

Lionel grimaced.

Sarah patted his hand. "Babe is great company."

"I sure hope so. She seems to like me," Lionel said.

"Definitely," Sarah said.

"But will she fly?" he asked.

Babe was under the trees near Sarah's terrace, playing with Ben who, along with the other crocodiles, felt and looked real and could speak intelligently and with appropriate emotion on a nearly limitless number of topics, thanks to immediate updates to their compbrains from headquarters and a built-in ability to learn.

"Weather pleasant tomorrow until evening. Squalls possible offshore after five PM," Ben announced. "Come here, Babe—good girl, good girl."

The crocodiles knew which animals, residents, Living Treasures, administrators and employees were certified to be at Pine Haven. Upon arrival by skimplane, a visitor's identification was instantly programmed into the robots' brains and then deleted when they left. A record remained in Administration Data for future match-ups and reports. The crocodiles quickly surrounded anyone who got onto the island another way—swimming, by private boat or plane—and would then bring the intruder to the Administrators, a three-person alternating committee, trained and appointed by the Prolocutor of Heaven.

"Oowee!" Ben called in his husky voice. That was the clue for Babe to find him. A difficult task, because although Ben was twelve feet long and one and one half feet wide, he had no smell and his green-black skin blended with the algae dotting the canal water, the moss under the wisteria trees and the broad leaves of the foundation planting near the administration dome.

Sometimes, he hid beneath one of the docks on the bay side of the island, or in plain sight in the deep shade of the dining hall. It often took an hour for Babe to trip or swim over him. She barked and leaped about afterwards, then climbed on Ben's back for a meandering ride to the ocean, where Ben watched her swim.

"Not too far," he warned. "Be careful."

After Lionel left, Sarah shaded the outer walls of her house by saying "darker" until the hue was right. No one could see in, even when the walls appeared translucent, but ever since Jeff died, she had preferred the look of absolute privacy. She could also change the appearance of her interior walls or furniture by looking in the direction of the object and murmuring a color. She'd been saying "pink" a lot lately, as recommended by her Angelic, Melody. Melody had promised to be with her at the last, to administer the elixir and hold her hand as Sarah had held Jeff's. Meanwhile, she had to prepare for the Celebration. Her children, grandchildren, great grandchildren and the only great-great grandchild born so far would be there.

Except for carefully monitored glitterplane races and water sports, residents weren't allowed off the island, and since Jeff's Celebration, she'd only had a few visitors, and this would be a grand reunion for the whole family. It would be fun, just as Jeff's had been. Every Sunday morning, she interacted with his Celebration Memory disk and made plans for her own, but this Sunday, Babe was supposed to go for a ride in the old duoplane with Lionel. The dog would be more likely to take to the air if Sarah were watching and waving from the beach. She'd have to go into Jeff's Memory later than usual.

Tomorrow, Saturday, she would spend time at the library. Maybe she'd get an idea in one of the seldom-read books.

At Departure Plaza, three Finals lay on gurneys, ready for

placement in the waiting aerohearse. If families wanted a religious service performed, they could claim their Final immediately after death. Shipping and handling would be at their own expense and the families were required to initiate the paperwork six months in advance of their loved one's Departure date.

Melody Graves stamped the Finals' cards and then filed them in a cabinet, an old-fashioned routine that had proved useful in 2066 when a space surge intercepted the electronic picture and printout of the records for an entire week. Using the hand-filed information, the Administration was able to recall the correct bodies for scanning one more time. This was possible to do because Finals kept forever and didn't require cremation or burial. The elixir that released them from life also eternally embalmed them, preserved their looks and made them pliable and light enough to carry.

Pine Haven, one of the smallest HEAVENs, had one of the largest facilities for Finals east of the Mississippi and it was prearranged each day for Zack, the resident pilot, to pick up additional bodies, at other facilities every afternoon so that counting the Pine Haven decedents there would be a total of six to fill the aerohearse to its maximum—although on occasion there were too few or none. It was then his responsibility to transfer them to the Plaza slabs for Melody to scan and match to the identification data collected when they came to Pine Haven or another location. Afterwards, she attached a bracelet around their ankles embedded with their history and identifying number.

Finally, either Melody or Zack secured each of them inside the aerohearse. Once loaded, Zack steered the plane to the adjacent airfield, flew to the mainland, landed and taxied down into the StrataDrome, a vast underground facility where thousands of Finals resided side by side on closely hung shelves. There he put them on custom-made eleva-wheels for placement later by one of the custodians.

Those tasks completed, this aspect of Melody's work for HEAVEN was finished for the week. She was always exhausted and hot on Fridays but looked forward to one of her three evenings of guaranteed free time. She was on call the other evenings for her regular resident-clients and others whose personal Angelic was away on a Diem.

National celebrations of religious holidays had been outlawed and replaced with four Carpe Diems per citizen. These could be claimed at any time with two weeks' notice and named whatever the citizen pleased to celebrate anything or anyone or nothing at all. Time off was arranged as always through employers. Virtual schoolrooms made it simple for children to be absent on days claimed by their parents. Religious songs could still be sung in places of worship, but the lyrics of all popular carols, anthems and marches had been changed to fit the no-differences agenda of the nation.

God bless America. Land that I love, for example, was now *Goods bless America, Things that I love*, which the no-differences agenda committee and sub-committees praised for being nearly indistinguishable from the original.

In three hours, Melody would be singing across the bay in the old city of Swyannah with the CrossOvers, a four-piece band capable of performing many musical styles. Every month, they honored a different historic period in popular music. Tonight they were beginning Country & Western.

As soon as Melody reached her room, she had a standing foam-bath, followed by a full cream session smelling of lily, her favorite flower and scent. She stuck her head in her pearlite niche for a two-minute simufinger massage, instant cleanwell drywash and precalculated hairplacement blow, then put on her new outfit—cowboy boots, short fringed skirt, rawhide jacket and, as she told her sister, "the sweetest little cowboy hat you ever saw."

Singing was the only thing she looked forward to since Roy had dumped her three months ago for Tessa Posnoff, a sex specialist with light amber skin, dark red hair and gold-green eyes. Tessa made good money at the Sex Center because of the tips from the many satisfied HEAVENLIES who could withdraw money from their small HEAVEN accounts or use the cash some received from their families. The Sex Center was by far the most popular place to go in the compound. Most residents had standing appointments with their favorite eroticist.

Melody wanted to attend classes for sex certification, but they were costly and it sometimes took years for a position to open up, unless she was willing to switch to another compound. There were thousands of HEAVENs now—some floating, some on mountains, some at lakeshores, a few near cities and many on islands.

But Melody had grown up at the beach and never wanted to be so far away that she couldn't hear the ocean. Also, the Pine Haven Island facility was close to her parents, who still lived in the cottage she grew up in. Zack found a way to give her a lift there and back whenever she got homesick.

She longed to have children, which meant she had to find a companion who was willing to sign the child-financial and nurturing forms. She had discussed it with Roy a few times. He loved kids, or so he claimed. At this point she wouldn't take him back even if he got down on his knees and begged to have one-point-five or even two kids with her, but it would kill her if he contracted to have children with Tessa.

Just the thought of it got Melody agitated. Emotion had a strong effect on her. Her face flushed, her stomach churned and she often murmured the beginnings of songs into her necklace insta-mem thought-retriever. When she thought of Roy, she felt sick to death.

"Love got mean; bit me in the heart,
Love last seen said I wasn't smart—
Well, I knew that, Hell, I knew that
I had the brains to know that."

She whispered it one more time, then belted it out to the mirror. "Jesus, that's good," she said to herself. "I need to finish that one later."

The sound of her voice made Melody feel better. "I'll make that Roy so effing sorry," she said. She looked in the mirror at her reflection: black wavy hair, cream-with-a-splash-of-mocha skin, upcurving blue-gray eyes.

"Damn, girl," she said to her mirror image. "Roy can go to hell. Someone's coming soon who will appreciate you. I can feel it. Your luck is changing. It has to, honey, because you're not rich enough to look like this forever."

Flushed and churning, she whispered:

"When your luck's about to change and for the better,
You can feel it, you can smell it;
When a light comes down and starts to shine around
you,
You can see it, you can tell it;
So you see it and you tell it.
Do I see it? Yeah. Do I tell it? Yeah.
Like it is."

"Not bad," Melody said, after singing as if to the balcony. "May finish that one too."

Melody had been born Mildred, the name given to the first female child of every generation on her mother's side since the eighteen-hundreds. She was nicknamed Melody because as soon as she could speak and say little nursery rhymes, she made up tunes to go with them. Later, when she wrote her own words, she did the same thing. Her parents told her she would be famous one day. She pretended not to believe them, but when she had tried out for the CrossOvers two months ago and gotten the job, she took it as a sign. Before you knew it—Huxley, the bandleader, would let her sing her own songs.

It was close to three months since Roy had started screwing Tessa. A big mistake, he now realized, especially since Melody's face was pushing into his mind again. If he decided to have children, she was the best candidate so far—but considering the way he'd treated her, there was no chance she'd talk to him, much less take him back. But what the hell. As it turned out he didn't need either of them. He always forgot what a nuisance women were until one of them was holding onto him too tight. The problem was how to let Tessa know their relationship was over so she didn't create a scene.

She wouldn't go quietly. Nothing she did was quiet. He used to like her orgasmic screams—they were a huge turn-on, especially when she came before he did, but not anymore. Like nearly everything else about Tessa they had grown to annoy him. He wanted to tell her to shut the fuck up. Did she want the neighbors to omniplus the police? Sometimes, he thought she was faking—not the orgasms, just the screams.

And let's face it, even if he was still crazy about her, he could never have introduced her to his family. His mother wouldn't see any difference between Tessa's position as a sex specialist at Pine Haven and a practitioner of the oldest profession. He supposed his mother might not be far off the mark. From what he'd heard—though it had to be an exaggeration—Tessa had slept with half of HEAVEN's employees, not to mention a good percentage of Swyannah residents.

Tessa was waiting for him, sipping vodka with a twist at a table on the deck of The Clam Shell, a hut near the skimplane landing in Swyannah. Roy had Wilbur with him, his new companion robot—a six-inch replica of Ben, except for his color, which was bright green, and his talent, which was tiny. He was designed only to download and play music, and record conversations.

"Hey Tessa! Say hello to Wilbur, my new best friend." Roy sat next to Tessa. He put Wilbur on the table. "Is he cute or what?"

Wilbur played some music, reared up on his hind legs and danced, his red mouth lip-synching the words of a 2063 ballad Roy liked.

"I swear you like your damn robots better than people. Tessa leaned over and tried to kiss him.

"Maybe."

"Did anyone ever tell you you're a control freak?" She nuzzled his nearest shoulder.

"Maybe."

"One of these days, you're going to design a robot so smart it'll be a mile ahead of you."

Roy frowned.

"Oh, sweetheart, I'm not serious." She jumped up, pushed the table away, sat on his lap and kissed his ear.

"Tessa! For the love of God! Someone could walk out here any minute."

"You never used to mind," Tessa said.

"Well, I do now."

Tessa got up and smoothed her hair. She swallowed the rest of her drink and tossed the ice into the canal. "Never mind, honey," she crooned. "You're just in an end-of-the-week funk. So am I. Who knows why?" She sighed. "We'll make everything all right on Sunday. Three o'clock at the dock. I'll bring glasses and a blanket; you bring the intoxofloat. We need to celebrate and talk."

"We can talk now," Roy said.

"Oh, stop. You know perfectly well Sunday is our anniversary—it'll be three months since we first made love there."

If he and Tessa did anything twice, the second time was an anniversary of the first time. He needed more than an enhanced omniplus to keep track of them all. And what he once thought was endearing was now making him want to choke her long, lovely neck.

She bent down to whisper in his ear, her tongue flicking its lobe. "I can't help it if I'm sentimental."

"I see. Well, fine. Terrific. It's a date. We definitely have to talk." Roy forced a grin.

"Right," Tessa said, and returned to her seat. "And hey, hon, please don't bring Wilbur, okay? He makes me nervous. I feel like he's eavesdropping."

"Gotcha," Roy said, without adding, from now on, wherever I go, he goes.

It was another kind of anniversary for Roy. Fourteen years earlier, his prototype of a robot crocodile to protect the residents of Pine Haven had been accepted by the Administration, and he was hired. He wouldn't have remembered the date, but his annual contract had arrived that morning with a letter thanking him for his ongoing contribution and offering the usual three percent wage increase that he always accepted without quarrel. The bonus of free lodging, meals and a state-of-the-art laboratory had made him loath to make a fuss. Also, his life was pleasant and without pressure and he had time to invent what he wanted using materials paid for by HEAVEN.

According to his contract, he retained the patent on all of his creations, past, present and future. His latest invention, the snoop-op, was going to make him famous and rich. And, he could come and go as he pleased in his custom heliozoomer, which HEAVEN permitted him to park on its airstrip.

He remembered the excitement of winning out over nine other roboticians who, in turn, had cut some two hundred. The criteria for the prototype robot were: it must be lifelike; able to talk; have upgradeable artificial intelligence; be able to reason and act sensibly after reasoning. And it had to knock their goddamn socks off.

Ben was more than anyone on the committee could have imagined; he was more than Roy himself had imagined. The other six robots, created later, didn't quite measure up to Ben, but they more than met the criteria.

Swyannah was five minutes from the island by skimplane. There was no tunnel or bridge across the bay to the city, so the only other choices were to swim or rent a boat or plane. The old part of Swyannah, approximately two miles square, where Melody was headed, was closed to all traffic except between the hours of five and eight A.M. when deliveries and garbage removal were allowed. The garbage was then transferred to AlChem, a government program, where it was turned into energy using the energy previously created by older garbage, a technique developed by a team of young, green-minded geniuses at I.I.I., the Institute of Immaculate Invention.

Before this solution, large areas of Louisiana had been set aside so that non-recyclable fill would slowly create rolling hills covered with grass and indigenous wildflowers where land was the flattest and where profits from the sale of its carefully monitored side effect, methane gas, would be used to restore levees and dikes.

After eight A.M., everyone walked or rode in a carriage. Melody loved it. Her parents had often brought her and her sister there when they were children, and little had changed since, except a few more stores and restaurants had opened while others had closed. The same had been true for her parents and great-grandparents.

It was a city lush with greenery all year, overrun with clematis, wisteria, magnolias and azaleas in the spring, some of which bloomed again in the summer or fall, and vast plantings of roses, day and Asian lilies nodding their many-hued heads throughout. The marriage of scents caused residents and tourists alike to forget what they planned to do and instead, sit on a bench or lean against a hanging cypress and think of other times to which their reminiscing noses guided them.

When Melody went back in memory, it was always to her grandmother's garden where she sat in the lap of a gray, sparkling rock, inviting and as big as a sofa, while her grandmother gathered flowers. Now she was at a time of life when a man might describe Melody herself as a flower, an orchid perhaps, rivaling the botanical varieties, but no such person was likely to turn up at The Come And Get It Café to hear her sing *Careless Love, Coal Miner's Daughter* or *I Fall to Pieces.*

Melody stepped off the skimplane, waved goodbye to the driver and hummed her way down one street and then the next and the next.

Melody hadn't realize how trapped she had felt until right then. "Thank you, Lord," she whispered.

Oh, I sound just like my granny, she thought. *Praise the Lord. That's what she always said. Oh, she'd kill me if she knew I haven't been to church since Easter.*

Oooh, Granny, are you watching me? I know damn well you are. Stop it, please. I'm doing the best I can. What I want to know is when am I going to meet the right one? You said there was a lid for every pot, but it's different now. Hardly anyone gets married; they just sign papers so both are legally responsible for any children who are born. Most of the time, the woman still takes care of the kids. Not such a hot deal, is it?

The few guys I've met who want a home and family are with somebody already, and they wouldn't say no to something on the side. It's sad, and the saddest thing of all is I was fool enough to fall in love, whatever that is, with Roy. I gave myself to him, heart, body and soul. Oh, it hurts so bad. The worst part is—I was too dumb to know he'd dumped me until I saw him out with Tessa and he didn't try to hide, didn't omniplus to say sorry, didn't give two cents.

"Jeez," she muttered. She'd been feeling great and now she was back to hating herself.

"Where's your boyfriend tonight?" asked Huxley, the lead guitarist.

Melody had no idea how he knew about Roy. It had been three months. Or maybe he was thinking of someone else, or maybe he was just fishing.

Her mother often pointed out that the truth was easiest as well as best. Or a half-truth? "We broke up."

"A mistake on his part, I'd say, Miss Melody." He smiled.

Was that a sarcastic smile? His mouth turned down on the left side. Hard to know. He always called her Miss. Was that sarcastic? She didn't think he liked her much.

"Thanks." She pulled the microphone from the stand. It worked but was also a prop. The act had to look—not just sound— authentic.

"From the top," Huxley said.

Huxley couldn't figure Melody out. There was a pale pink light around her and she looked so hot—the upcurving eyes, blood-red mouth, long, sculptured legs and round, sweet ass slowly waving or gyrating in front of him. She must know he was nuts for her. How come offstage she didn't give him the time of day?

He was accustomed to women responding quickly to his crooked smile and courtly manner. They didn't expect good manners from a guitarist, who was usually the sort to pinch your ass before saying hello and then act like you were lucky for the attention. But neither his smile nor manners seemed to do a thing to turn Melody on.

The night before, after their Country and Western grand opening, he expected they would get together for a beer, but when he took his eyes off the cheering patrons, the girl was gone. Never mind. If she wanted her wages, she'd have to talk to him after the Saturday performance.

Daily, after Huxley had his late breakfast, about the time many others in Swyannah were having a pre-lunch, watered-down old-fashioned, he taught guitar for a couple of hours, then made the rounds of the various houses under his care. Whether the owners were in residence or away, he was responsible to see the paper was picked up, the grass cut, beds raked, pool skimmed of bugs and leaves, animals fed, dogs walked and everything dry watered. He didn't do the actual work, of course; he hired people and oversaw them. He sent monthly bills to his employers, who paid well, in cash and off the books, and he paid the men and women out of that. He kept more than half. Sometimes, he was willing to house-sit so long as the employer understood he had weekend gigs and teaching appointments.

It was a great life in a great city and he'd been enjoying it with little variation for seventeen years. He was nearing forty and was proud to say he didn't own a house or a sunsonic, even though his savings account was hefty enough to buy both outright and still have a balance ending with double-digits and six zeroes. He was also proud to say he'd never been married, hadn't any children he knew of and was, according to the latest standards, in excellent health for a musician.

He believed he owed his happiness to following two rules—not to give a fig for what anyone else thought, and never to sleep with an employer. The latter wasn't an easy rule to keep, given his bad luck in bosses. Nearly all of the women were drop-dead gorgeous.

To maintain his successful record, it had many times meant running around a pool, a mass of shrubbery or a dining room table, with a half-naked woman in steady pursuit, singing out endearments.

"Oh sweet thing. Now you just stop and give us a kiss." Some were widowed or divorced, but he followed the rule nonetheless.

In order to keep such clients, he headed for home after each escape to write a note on fine paper bordered with hand-painted magnolias, explaining that although she was beautiful and desirable, he was, sad to say, gay. This meant he had to be up-to-date on the latest styles and colors in clothes, furnishings and flowers. He subscribed to several fashion and home and garden magazines to educate himself.

Consequently, the postman, and his landlord, both concluded he was indeed gay. There was no onus in being homosexual, but it caused problems when the landlord and later the postman came on to him. He told each of them that he was, sad to say, straight, and to explain his interest in the magazines, said he was studying to become a stylist. The mystery of this vague career fascinated his disappointed, would-be lovers and one or the other often cornered him with questions.

"Ah, that would be telling," he always said. Teasing was part of Huxley's acquired Southern charm, or what passed for it. Southerners were masters of the tease. Huxley's people were from San Della, a southwestern city featuring unvarying food, people and weather. No differentiation from one street to another and no place for an eccentric to flourish, which is what people told Huxley he was.

Huxley's mother, Harriet, was the one who told him Swyannah was the perfect little city for people like him, people who sang off-key, as she liked to say. She had a psychic aunt who had settled there and had lived out her days in perfect contentment. Aunt Edna died in the month and year she had predicted and out of doors, as she had also predicted.

She had told Harriet, she envisioned a ladies' luncheon al fresco where she would quietly exit this world following the syllabub. But no, she tripped over a small branch while crossing Peachstone Avenue on her way to a séance, and fell in the path of a horse drawing a carriage of sightseers. He shied, reared up and with a terrible whinny came down on Aunt Edna's head with both hooves. She was only eighty-three.

"She should have watched where she was going," Huxley's mother commented. "I hope they didn't kill the horse, poor thing."

They both flew east to Edna's funeral and Huxley, falling under the Swyannah spell, stayed on. Once a year, he returned to San Della, but now his mother, newly eighty-five, had moved to Pine Haven. He was relieved she'd agreed to come there so he could see her in her last years without him having to make the trip west.

Now, thanks to HEAVEN and his mother's compliance with the transfer of all her assets without tax to him, Huxley had more digits and zeroes in his bank account, and he had hired an agent to sell the San Della house and Harriet's valuables in order to add a few more.

"Don't you want to settle down with a nice girl and have a family?" his mother often asked, even though she assumed Huxley was gay. She thought it might get him to come out to her—besides, there wasn't a whole lot to say when they got together.

"I like things the way they are," Huxley always said, pursing his lips.

And what was that? His mother always wanted to know, but never asked.

One of these days, Huxley was going to ask her more about her life and especially about her husband, his father, the famous baseball pitcher, Huck Soong. Huck had died on the expressway on his way home from a game. Huxley was then eleven but had for years refused to throw, catch, or hit a ball. Huxley realized when he was an adult what a dreadful disappointment he must have been to this fast-running, muscular athlete blessed with such excellent hand-eye coordination that it transfixed the country, a veritable icon in the world of balls.

Huck was a mix of Asian, Indian and African-American, but none of the ancestors in those categories were true. They were mixed with various shades of white, from bone to puce to pale salmon and pink, since also hanging off his family tree were people from Ireland, England, France, Russia and Sweden, to name a few. Harriet's heritage was simpler, Polish, with a shot of Hispanic from her great-grandfather, an illegal immigrant.

Huxley couldn't figure out why Huck had married his mother. Except for a nice figure, jade-green eyes and a successful career as a psychologist, she wasn't anything special compared to his famous father, and she was fifteen years his senior to boot. The only explanation was that his father had actually loved her, been wild about her. Wow. It was almost impossible to believe. Huxley had never loved a woman in his entire life, though he'd screwed hundreds and planned to screw hundreds more. There was no longer any danger of AIDS or venereal disease as a consequence of the powerful vaccines of 2040 and 2047 so why the hell not? Plus it was his favorite thing to do, other than play the guitar. It was, in fact, his hobby and he practiced it, if possible, every day.

When he had visited his mother last week, Harriet was, for once, smiling when he arrived at her door for a Sunday visit. He was on time, shaved and generally looked like the sort of person his father would have found congenial.

"Hello, dear," she said and kissed his cheek. "How well you look."

"Thanks. So do you," Huxley said.

Harriet smiled.

"We could go for a walk before dinner," Huxley suggested.

"Okay," Harriet said.

"There's a great new Indian place. Want to try it?"

"I can't leave the island. Remember?"

"I forgot, but there's always take-out."

"I love a good curry. Since when are you so interested in food?"

"I've always had a good appetite," Huxley said. He was annoyed.

"You know what I mean."

"It's recent. Probably because I have your cookbooks and all that gourmet equipment."

"I'm surprised you kept any of it. Not many people cook anymore."

"Maybe that's why I do," said Huxley.

Later, Huxley remembered trying to make sense of the world by what grown-ups like his mother had said or did when he was little. Maybe that was why he'd never married. Maybe he'd sort of equated marriage with insurance policies and death. He wouldn't want a wife looking at him, knowing she'd be better off or just as well off if he were in an urn on her mantle. Not a chance.

"Would you look at that," Harriet said, indicating two crocodiles on patrol. "I haven't gotten used to them yet. They look so real." She shivered.

"One or two check me out every time I come over to see you and it's the same every time I leave. The security on the island is fierce."

"That's reassuring," Harriet said.

Huxley was silent trying to think of something to say. "Have you met anyone here you like?" he asked finally.

"You get mad when I ask you anything like that."

"I don't mean a guy. I mean people to do things with."

"Not yet. But I'm sure I will in time," Harriet said.

"You've been here a little over two weeks," Huxley reminded her.

"I was invited to play bridge with some women, but I don't like bridge."

"Okay. Well what about going to the Wisdom Center? You could learn a language."

"What for?" Harriet asked. "I'm not allowed to travel."

"For fun."

"Doesn't sound like fun to me, Huxley, dear." Then she added, "I'm suddenly quite tired. Let's go back, I'll fix you a quick drink and then if you don't mind, I'd like to lie down."

"What about dinner?" asked Huxley, surprised.

"I'll take a rain check."

Harriet could sense his irritation. He was easy to provoke. He was probably thinking she didn't understand him. Maybe not, but then he didn't understand her either. She was just trying to make conversation. *Now at least we'll have something to talk about*, she thought. She usually found their conversations strained; each struggling to find a topic that would interest the other. Cooking might be a thing they actually had in common. She had been an excellent cook years ago, but neither her husband nor son had been interested in what they ate as long as it filled them up and didn't taste unusual.

"What the hell is this?" Huck had asked her one evening when she'd sprinkled a small amount of minced cilantro on his broiled trout. "Tastes real funny." He made a face and doused the fish with salsa; he put salsa on everything but cereal and ice cream.

He'd been a good husband but, to her amazement, she had adjusted well to his death. He had been away from home so much that it didn't seem all that different, and the conservatively invested principal from his hefty insurance policy and considerable savings meant she and Huxley were set for a comfortable life, which her professional income would not have guaranteed. "Money may not buy happiness," she had told Huxley at that time, "but the lack of it brings misery. We need to thank your daddy for looking after us."

She was flattered when Huxley asked her to settle at Pine Haven. After all, he was her only child, conceived by mistake when she was forty-four and, once born, not at all what she'd had in mind, meaning he wasn't a thing like his father, whom she considered the perfect male template. Come to think of it, Aunt Edna had predicted Huxley would be different. "In a nice way and good-looking, so no one will notice much when he doesn't fit in," she had said. It wasn't till later that Harriet realized how important fitting in was to her, and how embarrassed she was when her son didn't conform. It wasn't something she would want anyone to know; it smacked of intolerance and she was proud of her reputation to the contrary. Aunt Edna hadn't stopped to explain that Huxley would simply not care what sort of impression he made on others, an admirable character trait, from Edna's point of view, since she didn't either.

Two weeks from now when he sees me, Harriet thought, *he won't know who I am.* The pictorials of what she would look like after her face and body were rejuvenated amazed her. She'd never looked that good in her whole life. *What a hoot this was going to be.*

SATURDAY, AUGUST 12, 2073

Sarah had always loved wandering around bookstores and libraries often with nothing specific in mind to buy or borrow. Today, she was looking for inspiration on how to escape Pine Haven. When Jeff was alive they'd always started in the history section. He had considered himself a student of the late twentieth and early twenty-first centuries in the United States—especially from the time the computer became essential to all grades of learning in all schools—nursery school included.

By the 2060's handwriting was no longer a requirement for graduation except that all students had to know how to sign their names, date a document and print certain facts if confronted by a form to complete by hand. By 2070, samples of outstanding penmanship from preceding centuries were framed, placed in museums as art and viewed with respect and amazement by the young. Retinal Identification (RI) or instant DNA matches were commonplace; pencils and pens were used only by notaries, artists and eccentrics. Crayons and paint were no longer favored; drawing was done onscreen.

Jeff had founded *Hands-on-Forever*, a group opposed to the demise of all things hand-written and hand-made. Sarah kept the cause going after Jeff's death, but it was difficult to find replacements for members who had resigned, died in the outside world, or Departed from HEAVEN. Younger people were accustomed to life without the need for nimble, artful hands. "Barbarians," Jeff would have called them. Sarah's last two

LimitLessLink letters had elicited no replies; she didn't plan to send any more.

Today, she headed for the how-to stacks, but because the HEAVEN residents had no reason to learn to do anything, there wasn't a great selection and absolutely nothing on how to escape, although there was a slim volume entitled *How to Do Almost Anything.*

She took it down and thumbed through the pages. She had learned to speed-read years before at the Wisdom Center and could take in a page in seconds, unless it was a page of poetry or literature deserving of slow mental ingestion. This book was worth borrowing, although she already had the gist of what it said: start where you want to be and work backwards, noting every step it took to get there in reverse. She'd give it a shot, though it sounded more applicable to advancing a career than escaping an island.

She went to the fiction section and pulled out *The Brothers Karamazov*, which she read every few years, just as her father had. It was an important book, her father had told her many times, perhaps the best ever written about human nature, and she wanted to read it once more.

Sarah was about to leave when she noticed a miniature of what looked to be a residential community. It covered a table near the back of the first floor where books deemed disagreeable or unnecessary to read were kept.

The rendering to scale was of Pine Haven. It was whittled of wood. Sarah asked the librarian on duty to follow her to the table.

"Who made that?" she asked.

The librarian shrugged. "No clue. I wasn't here when it was installed. It was on a Friday a few months ago and I'm off Fridays."

"It's exciting."

"Really?" The librarian looked doubtful.

"Made by hand. I mean, that's what's exciting."

"I see."

Sarah walked back and stood over the replica. Whoever whittled it was it was greatly skilled. *Who could it be?* Never mind. There wasn't time right now to find out. She needed to focus.

She checked out her books, walked outside and down the path toward her house

The problem wasn't just getting off the island. It was what she would do once she escaped—where she would go and how she would manage. Unless she could convince HEAVEN she was dead they'd never stop looking for her and how could she do that? Her body would have to seem irretrievable—lost in the depths of the ocean, vaporized in a hydrogen blast or incinerated in a fire of volcanic temperature.

Maybe Clarissa would help.

"Mother," Clarissa said from Sarah's ominplus, the delicate skin of her forehead creasing. "Surely I don't have to remind you that you brought us up to keep promises. And, my God, this is more than a promise. It's a signed agreement with the pluperfect United States government."

"I'm just not ready to die."

"You and dad said ninety-five good years would suffice."

"That's what we thought at the time."

"Don't you realize the government would take away everything you left us?"

"Only if they found out and even then it wouldn't be everything."

"You'd be sued for fraud so it probably would be everything."

Sarah sighed. *This wasn't going well.* "I thought you'd be happy if..."

"Mother," Clarissa said, her voice hard. "HEAVEN was your idea."

"No. It was your father's idea."

"Don't tell me he coerced you into this."

"Well, not really. Not entirely anyway."

Clarissa's mouth tightened. Sarah couldn't tell if she was annoyed or about to cry.

"Okay, give me some time to think about it," Clarissa said. "I hate that you're always changing your mind."

"What?"

Clarissa's face began to fade, then sharpened. "I'll have to discuss this with Barkley—it will affect him, too you know."

"Right. Barkley. Of course. Okay, Clarissa. We'll talk again soon. Goodbye."

Sarah pressed the omnipus to her sash where it clung as it did to any surface and went in for a nap. "Barkley," she murmured as she lay down. "Barkley." If Clarissa got him involved, there was no hope. She couldn't imagine her son going along with it. She was on her own.

Saturday night, Lionel left his house around nine in disguise: dark red-brown wig, thick eyebrows and beard, Stetson hat, jeans, a holster and boots. As an ex-senator and a Living Treasure, he was too famous to escape notice, and it was more fun to have women climb all over him as a tall, handsome somebody-else. He owned two-dozen custom-made wigs with matching eyebrows, mustaches, sideburns, chest hair, beards and goatees. His many outfits included those suitable for a visit to a Scottish castle in the eighteen hundreds, the high seas in the day of the buccaneers, the Wild West at the turn of the twentieth century, Hollywood in the nineteen-forties, Hollywood in the tens, Buckingham Palace when there was a monarch, and the moon in the thirties.

Twelve months earlier, the last time he'd worn a beard, he had gotten into an arm-wrestling match with a drunk that turned into a fistfight. And though neither party landed a punch, the drunk had fallen against the edge of a table, drawn blood and preferred charges. Lionel then had to reveal his identity to the police, who were as embarrassed for him as he was for himself.

"My advice, Senator Questar, sir," Investigator Krantz said, "is just be yourself."

"That's what my mother always said, Investigator, but now and then I feel like being someone else." Lionel had had a few tequilas.

"People are wary of beards, you know," Krantz said. "They wonder what you're hiding."

A year later, Lionel remembered Krantz's words and gave Ben, traveling as fast as he could beside him, his belated answer to Krantz's question. "Me, I'm hiding me. When you've lived a hundred years, you're tired of being you." They were on their way to the airstrip where Zack Dakota awaited him in Hoppy, Lionel's bright blue heliozoomer, his latest acquisition.

"Weather mild tonight with a high of seventy-five degrees," Ben proclaimed. "Nearly windless on the coast, picking up to ten offshore. Visibility, good to excellent."

"Thanks, Ben," Lionel said. "We should be back by two."

The crocodile backed off the airstrip and onto the grass, where he would lie and study human behavior on his compbrain until Lionel and Zack returned. Ben had recently enrolled in a doctoral program to earn his PhD in *Human Studies.*

Zack Dakota awaited Lionel inside Hoppy. Lionel didn't trust his own eyes to pilot the plane at night on his once-a-week evening jaunt, and besides, he liked having Zack with him while making the rounds. Zack played his part as Lionel's sidekick perfectly—he danced with the friend of any girl Lionel chose to romance, or made himself invisible until Lionel wanted him.

It was a great gig for Zack. He earned more money in one night with Lionel than he did in an entire week employed by HEAVEN. Because of Lionel, he had saved enough money so that as soon as he felt he could put two sentences together, he planned to say, "Melody, I love you. Marry me, please."

Then the two of them could start a new life away from the depressing work with Finals and about-to-be-Finals. Tonight, he decided to confide in Lionel.

"Senator, there's this girl I like. In fact, you could say I love her."

Lionel pursed his lips and raised his eyebrows. "Does she know?"

"Maybe. It's hard to say. I smile at her, she smiles back. Now and then on a Sunday morning, I fly her to visit her parents and then I pick her up in the late afternoon. She says thank you. I can hardly speak. I can hardly say goodbye."

"Chemistry," Lionel said.

"What?"

"Chemistry. That's what it sounds like. I married three times in the thrall of chemistry, so I know the signs. Nothing wrong with it. But eventually, you're sorry. Sick at soul. Bored. Thinking crazy thoughts. It's a terrible fact. Chemistry doesn't last."

"But she's my whole world."

"You must have read that somewhere."

"I believe we're fated to end up together."

"You read that, too," Lionel said.

"I shouldn't have told you," Zack muttered.

"Be glad you did. I may be able to save your life."

"Isn't that a little extreme?"

"Not a bit," Lionel replied. "Now, let's go have us a high old time. Feels like a five-city night."

Zack was beginning to seethe. So what if it was just chemistry? He didn't give a good hot damn.

Lionel loved the resort atmosphere where many people were open to talking to strangers. After an hour, if you mentioned the right names and places, such people would ask you to visit them next month at their lodge in the mountains. Couples think they're about to become your best friends, even though you're going to get up from your chair, say you'll be right back and never return. Single women don't invite you to their lodge in the mountains, you invite them to yours, not that you necessarily have one, then you take their reaches, get up and never return or omniplus.

Zack didn't approve. It offended his sense of right and wrong. He had been brought up to be truthful. But it was none of his business and the senator, after all, was paying him to drive Hoppy, keep his eyes averted and his mouth shut.

"What kind of example is he, anyway?" he mumbled, thinking of Lionel's marital track record and what Lionel had said to him about his feelings for Melody. Then a little louder, he added, "Who is he to give advice?"

"Sorry, did you say something?" asked a girl in a unikini. She had just walked by the palm he had half-hidden himself behind.

"Talking to myself," Zack said.

The girl smiled. "Wouldn't you rather talk to me?"

"Uh, well, maybe. I'm not a terrific conversationalist."

"I'm Annemarie."

"Hi."

What the hell was he going to say to her? She looked familiar but he couldn't tell her that.

She shivered.

"Say, are you cold?" Zack asked.

"A little. My suit's damp."

Zack noticed a redwood box full of towels by the pool. He jumped up, pulled one out and draped it around her shoulders. "See if this helps."

"That's so sweet. I mean," she said looking into his eyes, "really sweet."

"Come on. It's nothing," Zack said.

"Do you work, or are you independently wealthy, like most of the guys here?"

"Do I look independently wealthy?"

"I'd say so."

"Well, thank you, I guess, but I'm not. I'm a pilot. Weekends, I fly for him." He pointed to Lionel, who sat at a table, laughing, several women around him. "Now if you want someone who's independently wealthy, there's your man."

"I prefer you."

"Annemarie, you don't know the first thing about me."

"The point is I'd like to."

Lionel gave Zack the let's-go sign, which meant he had about a minute left. Too bad he hadn't met Annemarie earlier in the evening. She was easy to talk to and it was good practice.

"The trouble is I have to leave."

"That's okay. We can talk another time." She peered into her beach bag, dipped her hand in and brought it out holding a card. "Here's my reach. What's yours?"

She was so direct. He wasn't sure how he felt about that, but he scribbled his name and reach on an old flight schedule and handed it to her.

"Zack Dakota. Great name," Annemarie said. She smiled. She had a deep dimple in one cheek, gold-green eyes, skin shining pale amber. "If you don't contact me, I'll contact you."

"In that case," Zack said, "you'll hear from me soon."

Zack hoped Lionel hadn't been paying attention, but of course he had.

"Pretty girl," Lionel said, as they landed in Puerto Bono.

"Huh?" Zack said, pretending he didn't know who Lionel was referring to.

"That Annemarie."

"How'd you know her name?"

"I asked."

"Yes, she's pretty. So what?"

"Just stating a fact."

"She looked familiar," Zack said.

"After a while, they all do," Lionel said with a weary smile.

From Zack's point of view, Lionel had a way of spoiling everything. Did he mean to? Zack was beginning to dislike him. In the past, he had seemed too important a person for a guy like Zack to judge—he was a glorious monument of a man. Inviolate. Now, his arrogance, and especially his goddamn cynical perspective, made Zack want to punch him out, even if he was a big shot and a hundred years old.

A five-city night and at ten forty-five, Puerto Bono was only the second one they'd got to. How could they be back on the island by two o'clock? Maybe Lionel wouldn't want to stay here long. Maybe the crowd would be old, or worse, loud. Maybe there wouldn't be anyone interesting to talk to, no women circling him, which had never happened.

"Senator," Zack said, "take a look at the time. Do you really think we can hit three more cities tonight?"

"We've done it before."

"We started earlier," Zack said.

"Let's see how it goes. Why not try?"

Zack moved as far from Lionel as he could while still being in sight. He didn't want to take the chance of talking to another pretty girl. Annemarie had messed up his head enough. He felt as guilty as if he'd cheated on Melody, even though he knew he couldn't have because she didn't know he loved her, didn't know he went to bed with her every night—because in his mind, Melody and he had three children, several dogs, cats and a goat and lived in the mountains. There was no changing it.

What he'd have to do was reach Annemarie in the morning before she could possibly reach him and explain to her he was seeing someone else. Of course, that wasn't the truth, so he'd have to think of something to say that was.

Swyannah was their last stop. They had stayed over an hour in St. Miguel, Florida, and forty-five minutes each in Puerto Bono, Mexico; Yama Tama, California; and Targetville, Colorado. The trip time was negligible, thanks to state-of-the-art magnetic travel and valet hover-parking.

"Do you like Country & Western music?" Lionel asked Zack.

"Don't know. Never heard of it."

"Boy, it's part of your heritage, like swing, jazz, the blues, rock and roll, rap."

"Haven't heard of them either."

Lionel patted Zack on the shoulder. "You've been deprived, Zack. A great shame. Tonight, we'll see to it you get a good dose of old-time music."

They were already in front of The Come and Get It Café. Lionel peered closely at the show times in the glass-covered recess next to the entrance. "We're in luck. The last show's just started. Hoo ha. I'm ready." Lionel had already downed four tequilas, one at each stop and was looking forward to a fifth.

Huxley and the boys were in full swing, playing some bluegrass. When they finished, Huxley held the microphone as Melody danced out on the stage. He handed it to her.

"Hey there everybody," she called. "How *be* you?"

"Just fine," came the drawling answer from those who knew how to respond, which included Huxley, the band members, the café manager, three waiters, and Lionel, who had tried and failed to pull Zack down next to him at a round table in the back. Zack was immovable, stone-steady, his olive skin alternating between a yellow-orange and a puce-white.

"What the hell is the matter?" Lionel asked. "You sick?"

"No, Senator." Zack sighed, and after a long silence, after he was able to move, after he sat down and ordered a drink and after he looked in his mind for his wife and children and found them missing on the mountain, he explained, "Not sick. Just didn't expect Melody."

"Well, what do you know?" Lionel said. "I sure thought you had a tin ear—but since you know a pretty tune when you hear one..." He looked Zack in the eye and, with affection, patted him on the back. "I do believe there's hope."

"Shit," Zack said. "Hope is what I just lost."

"Huh?"

"Do you see that girl up there?"

Lionel nodded and looked at Zack like he was crazy.

"That's her. That's Melody."

Lionel raised his eyebrows.

"My girl, sort of. Don't you get it?"

Lionel shook his head.

"I didn't know she could sing and dance and who knows what all. Damn it to holy hell, she'll never look at me now."

SUNDAY, AUGUST 13, 2073

Early Sunday morning, when there were only three songs to go, Huxley gave the signal for the CrossOvers to take a short break, their second of the evening.

"Hey," Huxley whispered to Melody when she returned, "your paycheck will be waiting for you as soon as we finish."

"I thought it was going to be cash," Melody whispered back.

"It is. I was teasing."

"I'm getting a lift home from some friends so I can't hang around."

"You talking about the guy with the beard?" Huxley asked.

"He's one of them, yes."

"I believe he passed you a note when you went down to flirt with the crowd."

"My-oh-my, you notice a lot, don't you?" Melody didn't sound pleased.

"Just being protective, Miss Melody, honey. After all, you're my star."

Honey. Had he gone too far? She had a dignity about her he couldn't get beyond. And calling her a star when he, Huxley, was the star. She knew that. Damn.

Melody looked at him as if he'd said nothing out of line. "Why don't I just pick up my pay at rehearsal next Thursday?" she asked.

"Suits me," Huxley said. "What do you all say we finish the show?" He shot his crooked smile her way and nodded to the band.

"The Mississippi Waltz, my favorite," Melody cooed into the microphone.

"How my sweetheart and I loved to dance," she sang, *"to the Mississippi, Mississippi Waltz."*

Huxley was having a hard time concentrating. For certain, he wasn't lost in the music. She really had a luscious voice, but the body, oh—Good God Almighty— that body was exceptional, and Melody made it plain it wasn't up for grabs. She was a challenge, and Huxley hadn't had one in a long time. Maybe never.

Lionel fell asleep in one of Hoppy's two reclining chairs. His beard and wig were askew, nose crusted with dried blood, a dark-pink lump on his forehead.

Zack touched down near Melody's apartment and got out with her.

"I wouldn't have minded walking from the airstrip," she said, "but this is really nice. Thank you."

"You must be tired," Zack said, the booze and excitement helping release his tongue in Melody's presence. "All that singing and dancing."

"I enjoy it," Melody said. "It's not like real work."

"Let me know when you want to visit your parents again."

"I will." She smiled, leaned over and kissed Zack on the cheek. "You're a sweetheart," she said. "And please thank the senator for me. Glory, I had no idea that's who he was."

And she wouldn't have if it hadn't been for Lionel drinking one tequila too many and taking offense when a fellow at the next table made a lewd remark about Melody while she was singing *Coal Miner's Daughter.*

"What did you say, motherfucker?" Lionel had asked.

"Just so you know, Investigator," he said later to Investigator Krantz, "I gave him a chance to shut up, but he said it again. That's when I had no choice but to hit him."

"I guess he'll say he had no choice but to hit you back," the investigator said. "Didn't I tell you beards were trouble?"

"It's been a year. I needed to have some fun."

"Well you've had it and now I have to book you."

Zack was becoming agitated. "Investigator, I've got to speak up for the senator, sir. He would never have done what he did if he weren't defending the honor of the woman I love."

Krantz was taken aback. He seldom heard the word "love" used any more. He turned to Zack and asked in a respectful tone, "Your wife?"

"Not yet," Zack said.

"Your fiancée then?"

"Yes," Zack answered. "My fiancée." He had told a lie but what could he do?

"Well then," the investigator said. "That's different. Where is she now?"

"She's waiting for us, Investigator. We need to fly her home. Her parents are waiting." Another lie.

"I'd sure like to meet the woman a senator would risk his reputation for."

"You will. That's a promise," said Zack, not sure whether that was a lie or not.

Ben moved quickly to greet Lionel and Zack when they emerged from the heliozoomer at two forty-five. He had set his alarm for two o'clock and since it went off, he'd been worried about them. He had continued to download information on humans, but it neither informed nor distracted him. He could see right off that something was wrong, although as usual the senator said, "Hey, big guy, how's the weather down there?" Then only ten steps off the airstrip, he collapsed.

Both Zack and Ben groaned.

"We've got to get him to the hospital fast," Zack said. "He may have a concussion."

"No problem," Ben said. "Stretch him out on my back."

The dead weight of the senator was too much for Zack to lift.

Ben signaled emergency. "Should've done that to begin with," he said to Zack. In seconds, the red, glittering lights of the Medivan were headed straight toward them.

"Thank God," Zack said.

The Administration of Pine Haven was lodged in a round building made of blue synthoflex, half-surrounded by many-colored curved sections. From the air, they looked like consecutive rainbows over a blue circle, each separated by grass and matching curved slate promenades forty-five feet apart. Openings here and there allowed for hydrocars and the odd slim-truck.

The sections were all seventeen feet deep and divided into approximately eighteen-foot-wide apartment wedges for Pine Haven employees. They were sparsely furnished with a small interior entry leading to the sleep theaters and baths. There were no kitchens—it was possible to heat or freeze food in three-foot cubes also used for storage of perishables or extra seating. One of the many advantages of being employed by HEAVEN was that bed, board, uniforms, laundry and many other conveniences were provided. The employees enjoyed the same excellent medical care, not including organ or parts replacement, age displacement or overhauls of the brain, as did the residents, albeit on another floor of the hospital. Also, they were served the same food, or meal pills not including the Celebration banquet buffet, albeit in another dining room.

One of the original HEAVEN proscriptions was against the mixing of employees and residents, except during the performance of duties. When questioned, the Prolocutor said, "What would happen if you became really good friends with a resident whose Departure you had to facilitate?"

The rules were in an electronic booklet, which prospective employees were required to master. Before being hired, they had to pass a test. There was no test for residents but as soon as they arrived they were handed a booklet reviewing the legal agreement between them and the state. It began with a copy of their signed agreement. Next was the amendment:

Amendment XLI
Section 1. This article applies to all persons attaining the age of eighty-five who elect of their own free will to live until age ninety-five, and no longer. Such persons shall be cared for by the state until the age of ninety-five, or the next weekday following if said birthday falls on a weekend or carpe diem. At that time, the state will assist them to depart life without pain, and in a state of ecstasy. Such persons are permitted to bequeath their estates in total, without federal, state or local tax, to any designee(s) upon the start of their residency in any legitimate HEAVEN environ. No person shall elect to participate in HEAVEN if not of sound mind.

Section 2. This article shall be inoperative unless it shall have been ratified as an amendment to the Constitution by the legislatures of three-fourths of the several states within seven years from the date of its submission to the states by the Congress.

Section 3. The Congress shall have power to enforce this article by appropriate legislation.

Ratification was completed on February 3, 2058.

Later, it was proposed and enacted into law that a maximum of ten Living Treasures would be elected by electronic ballot on January first of every year. Any certified citizen could make a nomination, but in order to be in the running, each name had to be seconded five hundred thousand times, and verified by a hacker-proof satellite site carefully monitored by two qualified Senate committees. This meant that only the most famous politicians, celebrities, singers, musicians, authors, athletes and the like were chosen. Living Treasures had all the privileges of HEAVEN, but continued living as long as they liked or could. As an additional benefit, their spouses became Associate Living Treasures, with all attendant rights.

Lionel awoke. His head was clearer than it had been in a long time, maybe than it had ever been. It must be the new chips they'd slipped in to rejuvenate his gray cells while they fixed the damage from the fight at the café. He had found his surgeon's technical description of the prospective procedure horrifying and had refused to watch.

"Knock me out, for Chrissakes," he had said. "I don't like the sight of blood, especially mine."

It was now about eleven o'clock on Sunday morning, several hours after the operation. He lifted his head slightly.

Zack sat in a chair at the foot of Lionel's bed, legs splayed, head fallen back, mouth open, snoring.

"Well, what do you know?" Lionel whispered to himself, pleased.

The nurse, entered. "I thought you might be stirring," she said. She stared at the screen over his head. It showed an ever-changing read-out of Lionel's bodily data compared to his visuals and data from 2015 on.

"If we get your blood pressure down to normal, you may be able to go home tomorrow. We'll see how it goes. Are you hungry?"

"Maybe," Lionel grunted. "I just woke up."

"I'll have the aide bring you some toast and coffee."

"Him too?" Lionel pointed to Zack, who had just opened his eyes and was attempting to get his head up from where it hung backwards.

"Sure," the nurse said.

"Have you been here all night?" Lionel asked. He watched Zack's head rise slowly and arrange itself to sit upright and straight on his shoulders.

"I guess so."

"Thanks. What time is it?"

Zack looked at his watch. "Eleven fourteen."

"Uh-oh," Lionel said.

"What's the matter?"

"I'm supposed to pick Babe up at eleven-thirty."

"Who?"

"A dog I'm planning to adopt."

"Oh."

"Do me a favor—omniplus Sarah Rally and tell her I have to postpone the flight."

"Okay," Zack said. "What code?"

"Two blue, one red, six purple."

Sunday's early-morning fog burned off before ten o'clock. It was nearly time for Lionel to pick up Babe. Sarah hadn't slept well, worried the dog might not like flying and, if not, Lionel might decide not to adopt her after all. Only one other person had answered her ad—Sarah couldn't remember the name and it was too late to advertise again. Most residents had their pets Depart with them, but Babe's life expectancy was another ten years at least. She thought a relative would take her and had dropped hints for months to no avail. Babe deserved someone who treasured her.

Sarah had spent the morning with the past in her lap and on the floor—yellow pictures in albums, fragile clippings in boxes. Except for some furniture, books and her jars of diamonds hidden in thick face cream in case she needed them to start a new life, they were all she and Jeff had brought from their previous life to Pine Haven. Soon, Clarissa, her eldest daughter, would inherit and, finally, organize them.

Clarissa knew everyone's history and where people were when their pictures were taken. Sarah intended to give them to her after the Celebration, along with all the Memory disks.

"Sarah, are you there?" asked a voice from her omniplus.

"Uh huh," Sarah said.

"This is Zack, a friend of Senator Questar's. We've met a couple of times."

"Of course," Sarah said, standing up, memories spilling on the floor. "What's wrong?"

"Nothing much—a slight accident—but he'll be fine. He wanted you to know he'll have to postpone the date."

"That's fine," Sarah said. "But poor Lionel. Where is he?"

"In the hospital. He had a minor surgical procedure."

"What does that mean?"

"A small cerebral overhaul. Nothing major."

"That's a relief. When can he have visitors?"

"Tomorrow," Ben said.

Ben had positioned himself outside the hospital for the night. If he'd been shorter, the emergency nurses would have let him go upstairs with Zack to keep watch over—or in his case, under—Lionel, but his twelve-foot long body wouldn't fit into their largest elevator, and folding him up wasn't an option. His body was nearly a foot deep and stiff with hi-tech innards.

Although his size was occasionally a disadvantage, as a robot he would last forever, assuming regular parts updates or replacements, was weatherproof and didn't require sleep or food. However, he did require companionship and what he believed his friends would call love. Why he needed these two things was a mystery to him. The other robot crocodiles were diligent in their duties, but had no needs whatsoever. He'd been with them enough to be certain. Ben hypothesized that Roy, his creator, had stuck a speck of some human essence somewhere inside his compbrain. *Not worth worrying about,* decided Ben. *I am what I am.*

And people are what they are. But what is that? This question occupied his off-hours while he studied human behavior in the centers of information already resident in the one lobe of his compbrain. Everything in print, past and present, was there to read or, in his case, download into memory. Once there, it took time to absorb. Much about what people called the human race, he noted, was still unknown. His goal was to fill in some of the gaps. His thoughts were transferred into writing whenever he was, as he was fond of saying, "in the mode."

Ben had studied his prototype and that of other animals but couldn't identify with them. Hunger and procreation powered these creatures and both were concepts he struggled to understand. He decided hunger was analogous to missing someone he loved, the kind of feeling he had more and more when a friend was away or, as now, in the hospital.

The trouble with people is they were unpredictable and fragile, and worse—it didn't seem to bother them. Nothing about Lionel, the dignified senator and Living Treasure, whose public life Ben had studied at length, prepared him for Lionel's collapse following his exit from Hoppy. He'd been leaning on Zack, three-quarters his size, for support. Lionel's blood had coagulated on his forehead and nose, but was still oozing from the back of his head, on which he'd fallen, but he, nevertheless, had hummed *"Side by Side"* with an occasional misremembered lyric, "we may be a barrel of monkeys," as if nothing were amiss.

Ben knew music and lyrics inside out, all the way back to the Elizabethan days, and was particularly fond of American show tunes of the twentieth century, though he made no attempt to hide his prejudice in favor of the English in other ways. He spent a good two hours a night listening and singing along, as quietly as possible, to his favorites. If he'd been human, he believed he would have been a performer, the kind who gave concerts and had fan clubs. He might have played an instrument, but which one? He loved the piano, but he couldn't imagine himself fingering the glorious eighty-eight with finesse. The drums were a more likely fit.

Melody woke up Sunday morning, thinking of Lionel. She was flattered to know that a man of his prominence had actually gotten into a fight to defend what used to be called her honor. Of course, he'd been drunk, but still—what a fine gentleman. There weren't decent men around like that anymore. He was old, but if he truly loved her, what difference would that make? She would rejuvenate him—make him happier than he'd ever been in his life. If he truly loved her, that is. Somehow, it went without saying that if he did, then she would truly love him back.

If, on the other hand, he was just being gallant, thought she was a sweet, innocent kid, maybe he'd help her break into the music industry. Maybe he'd introduce her to some big-time important people, maybe he'd back her first song, and maybe he was the answer to her years of ambitious dreams.

Of the two scenarios, she liked the second one best.

The challenge was how she could find out what was in Lionel's heart or brain or soul—wherever he kept his intentions.

"I'm here, Senator," Melody said, as if he'd been expecting her.

"So you are," Lionel said, "and looking pretty as ever." He winked at Zack. "Isn't she?"

Zack nodded.

"Hi, Zack," Melody said. "What's the report?"

"They say he's in great shape now."

"Now?" Melody asked.

"What Zack means is that my brain has been upgraded and I've never felt better in years, except for a temporary, or so they tell me, headache," Lionel said.

"Lord, the things they can do. It's wonderful," Melody said.

Zack stared at her.

"Senator," Melody said, sitting on the nurse's stool. "I'm so sorry you were injured on my account."

"What do you mean?"

"Oh Senator," Melody said. "You belted the fellow who insulted me."

Hearing this made Lionel worry. He was afraid Melody was going to be grateful, and there wasn't anything more exhausting than a woman's gratitude. She would spend too much time thinking of nice things to do for him, and then she would do them. For all he knew, she had fallen in love with him already, because in his experience, that's one of the things women did when they were grateful.

He still loved to flirt but no longer was interested in the complications that went along with women. He'd had enough. He wanted to fly, read his books and play with his dog, once he had her. From now on, he was staying out of other people's business, and this business belonged to Zack. If Zack didn't know how to carry on, it was too damn bad.

Now, two hours later than usual, having changed her routine for Lionel, Sarah put Babe on what she called the porch, a narrow, airy, wraparound room so that she could play Jeff's Celebration disk, enter the Memory and dance with him again.

Sarah selected a Memory disk from the cabinet and placed it on a tall silver pedestal in the middle of the main room. "On," she said. A mother-of-pearl globe of light enveloped the pedestal. It ballooned out and when it touched her, she stepped in. The Memory surrounded her and she was back to March 2, 2071.

Sarah looked for Jeff. He usually stood waiting for her just inside, and together they would follow the music to the dance floor. Today, the music was faint and the hallway she chose to walk down led her to another and another and another, and finally to a blank wall. So back and back and back she went, and then down another hallway and around to where at last the music got louder, and she found a glass door leading to an enormous room filled with her children, grandchildren and friends who had come to Jeff's Celebration.

She passed her son, Barkley, doing a Simon Says dance with his wife. "Hi," she said and blew them each a kiss.

"Where's your father?" she asked Clarissa.

"Last time I saw him, he was dancing with that attractive redhead from the Center," she said.

"The Sex Center?"

"He didn't say, Mom."

Had this happened before? Every visit was a little different from the ones before because, she finally figured out, she visited another part of the Celebration each time. Also this time she had arrived later than usual but she definitely didn't remember Tessa coming to Jeff's Celebration, taking part in the Memory. Tessa was the eroticist Jeff always asked for at the Center, but it was different when Sarah was with them in the space of sex. Tessa was there to stimulate them until they were both in the mood, then close the curtain so she and Jeff were alone. At that time, Sarah had still been interested in sex, especially when she drank a libido-mango cocktail first.

Now she wondered if Jeff had been going to the Sex Center without her before his Departure. For months he had said he needed a long walk alone to prepare for the upcoming nothingness. It happened every afternoon after lunch.

"There won't be nothingness, Jeff," she'd told him. "And even if there is, how can you prepare for it?"

He hadn't answered.

It hit Sarah that he'd been using his pending Departure as an excuse to visit Tessa. The more she thought about it the more convinced she was. He'd acted guilty; he'd gone for his walk every afternoon at exactly the same time. She felt sick to her stomach. To think he had lied to her at the very end of his life. It was unforgivable. It ruined everything. She sat at a table near the crowded dance floor. To think at long last, she had trusted him again. What else had he lied about? There was no telling.

Meanwhile this wasn't anything like the Memory she remembered. There were new hallways and spaces and someone who wasn't there before but was there now. Maybe she was in the wrong Memory. But no, there was Jeff. Sarah waved to him and, out of habit, smiled.

"There you are!" Jeff reached for Sarah's hands, drew her up and out of the chair into his arms. He was a large, powerful man, over six feet tall, weighing two hundred pounds. "You're late."

She pushed him away.

"What's the matter?" he asked, following as Sarah walked onto the terrace overlooking the beach.

"I suppose that explains why you didn't meet me. I got lost, you know. There were hallways I'd never seen before," Sarah said.

Jeff tried to take her hand. Sarah moved farther away.

"I understand you were dancing with Tessa, everyone's favorite specialist."

"Who said so?" Jeff asked.

Sarah expected the question. "Oh, Jeff, I didn't need to be told—I know what you've been doing, and are about to do." *Was his face flushing?* "And with whom."

"What?"

"Every afternoon for two hours."

Jeff turned away.

Oh, my God—he wasn't going to deny it. "I thought we told each other everything," Sarah said.

"Sarah, Sarah," Jeff said.

She hated it when he repeated her name in that reproachful tone as if she were a difficult child. "Oh Jeff, it ruins everything, everything I believed about our lives together these last fifteen years."

"Sarah, Sarah."

She wanted to hit him.

"There's nothing between Tessa and me," he said. "If that's what you think."

"You mean—you're not going to see her anymore?"

"What?"

"Next week. Every day before your Departure."

"I don't know what will happen then. I don't want to think about it."

"Why is Tessa here now? She wasn't before."

"Of course she was."

"Why didn't I see her?"

"How the hell do I know?"

"I'm sorry; Jeff, but I don't believe you. You always know everything."

Sarah kicked off her shoes, threw them under a chair near the pavilion and ran down the stairs to the beach where she landed hard, the rocks scraping the bottoms of her feet, and on to where her soles got so hot she ran even faster to bury them in the wet, soft sand cuffing the ocean. She watched her footprints disappear again and again with the tide. She was spoiling Jeff's Celebration. It would never be the same. Well that was too damn bad.

"Oh, it's so rotten—I hate him!" she cried out, her fury overwhelming her. Jeff always said she turned into a drama queen when she was upset. "I'll drama-queen him," she muttered. "I'll drown myself!"

Crazy, but why not? She was going to die in two weeks anyway, and her own upcoming Celebration would only remind her of Jeff and Tessa. Ha! This could be the moment that would make her famous. She'd go down in history as the first resident of HEAVEN to commit suicide.

She'd read that drowning was a pleasant experience, once the bad part was over, and that didn't last long. The question was—could she drown herself in Jeff's Memory space over two years in the past? It might not be possible. She might be invulnerable. But it was worth a try. She looked back toward the pavilion. No one was on the terrace. She waded into the rippled ocean, the noise of the party in her ears.

Twenty minutes later, when Jeff returned to the terrace with Tessa in tow, he was surprised not to find Sarah in plain view still cooling her feet. He wanted Tessa to explain that nothing sexual had ever or was about to take place between them, that Sarah's suspicions were without merit, that in fact, Tessa was leaving Pine Haven to take a position with a HEAVEN installation in the mountains for a change of scene.

Only the last part was true, or partially so, but it was important for Sarah to believe it all for her peace of mind, and for his. What was true was that Tessa had fallen for Jeff, and he for her. They had been sleeping together in her apartment for months and would continue to do so until his Departure. Tessa would leave Pine Haven after Jeff's Departure, not for a change of scene but to get over Jeff.

"She can't have gone far," Jeff said.

"You can see a good mile in either direction," Tessa said. "So where is she?"

"Maybe she came back in. Wait; let me see if her shoes are still here."

They were.

"She wouldn't, would she?" Tessa asked.

"Only," Jeff said, "if she were really pissed."

"Uh oh," Tessa said.

Jeff shielded his eyes with his hands and looked out to the ocean. "Sweet Jesus," Jeff said. "I see something."

"What?" Tessa asked.

"Where are the lifeguards? They're supposed to be on duty!"

"I think I saw Tom a few minutes ago in the bar," Tessa said.

"Hurry," Jeff said.

It's not as if Sarah hadn't done some damn-fool things before. She'd been a sensible, easygoing person most of their marriage, although from time to time, she'd reacted in a way he couldn't have predicted. But this was the first suicide attempt, if in fact that's what it turned out to be.

Thirty-seven years ago, she had left the house with her largest pocketbook and smallest duffel bag, gotten into her Abudi and driven off without a word. She didn't return for two weeks. They'd had a fight. He never found out where she went. For all he knew, she'd had a boyfriend. So what was all that about telling each other everything, telling each other the truth? Of course he didn't tell her the truth—the truth ruined everything, which is why he didn't tell her. He had taught himself to deny troublesome facts and keep on denying them. It worked. Usually. Just not this time, or at least not so far.

Sarah was able to walk waist-high for what she estimated was a half-mile or more. It was going to be hard to drown in such a placid, shallow sea. Where was the unexpected giant wave? Where was the undertow? And, more importantly, where was her anger? The effort of walking against water had tired her, and at the same time dissolved her fury. She'd also had some time to rethink the situation between Jeff and Tessa.

What did it matter what they did or didn't, would or wouldn't do? It was all in the past. She was furious but there was no changing it. The present was outside this Memory with her family and friends, Lionel, Melody, Babe and Ben. Babe! How could she even think of suicide? Also, she had promised Lionel she'd come to see him in the hospital tomorrow. Sarah turned around. What a relief. A green slitherboat was coming quietly toward her with Tom, her favorite lifeguard, in the driver's seat.

Hey, Mrs. Rally," Tom said, a grin making deep ridges in his cheeks. "Just where were you headed?"

"Marseilles," Sarah said. "It's shallow enough."

"The sharks might have had other plans."

"I didn't know there were any."

"Now you do," Tom said.

"Thanks for coming for me."

"Your husband spotted you. Let me give you a hand."

"I'll need more than a hand, Tom." Sarah was, at the moment, feeling extremely old. Never mind that she didn't look it.

He lifted her onto the boat as if she were as light as the seaweed clinging to her clothes.

"Sorry for the trouble," Sarah said. She felt the urge to explain, but resisted. What was the point? This, too, was in the past, even though it had just happened.

Jeff and Tessa waited on the shore. Tom pushed onto the sand as Jeff bounded to the boat, helped Sarah out and festooned her with towels.

"You'd better hop into a hot bath as soon as you get home," Jeff said. "You don't want to get pneumonia."

"Under the circumstances, who cares?" Sarah said. "I didn't realize I'd walked out so far. But you're right—I'm freezing to death. I guess I'd better get going."

"Wait, Tessa wants to talk to you."

"Why would I believe anything she said? Never mind. It doesn't matter I mean—I really don't care anymore." *Such a lie.*

Jeff looked shocked.

"You don't need to walk me out, Jeff," Sarah said. "I'll be fine. Goodbye." She kissed his cheek. "Enjoy the rest of your Celebration."

Shoes in hand, Sarah padded her way out of the pavilion into the various halls and toward the Memory curtain beyond.

I should have reminded him he'd be dead in a week—his time, she thought. *But then, so will I, in a little over a week—my time.*

Or not. She still had her rainy-day security and how-to book.

Harriet underwent all of the procedures developed in Argentina, perfected in Hungary and long available to the superrich: non-stop colored light therapy that regenerated her protoplasm and skin and internal upgrades so that her insides were in perfect working order, "comme il faut," as her doctor-for-oversight observed. Her hands were plumped and without age spots, her legs were smooth, the varicose and spider veins gone, her breasts were pert, the curtains under her arms had vanished, her entire epidermis was clear of wrinkles, her buttocks, thighs and calves firm and smooth as marble, no cellulite anywhere.

She was sprayed head to toe with an everlasting tan programmed to copy itself onto new skin. Her neck was slim and tight, and her face completely redone through atomic surgery. Her nose had a lilt, her lips curved into a smile when in repose; her mouth was full and no longer outlined with a hundred tiny rays. Her eyes were bright, long and sultry, no crow's feet, no loose lids, no bags. Her hair had been cut, restyled and lightened. She was more than attractive—she was a total knockout.

Huxley, as she had predicted, didn't recognize her when she opened the door to his worried face. Harriet had contacted him in tears and asked him to please come as soon as he could. In her hand were two damp tissues, which she pressed to her eyes. Her rings gave her away, a diamond engagement ring and platinum and diamond wedding band flanked by sapphire guard rings.

"My God, Mother," Huxley said.

"I know."

"What happened?"

"I had the complete do-over, inside and out. I should have had more sense."

Huxley collapsed into the oversized club chair she had brought from home especially for him. "It's going to take a while to get used to you."

"Ditto," Harriet said. "I feel like a fool. No one will know who I am." She laughed. "Including me."

"At least you didn't make many friends here."

"True."

"Cheer up, Mother. You're beautiful."

"I thought it would be wonderful but I don't like it. I don't know who I am anymore." She sat on the couch.

"You're still the same person."

"I wish."

Huxley was trying to make her feel better, but he didn't think she was the same person either. Her aura had changed. She'd gone from pale gray to lavender-blue.

The terrible thing was, and he would never tell anyone this, he found his own mother attractive. If he didn't know who she was and had seen her under other circumstances, he might have hit on her. No, not really—but yes, possibly. It was the strangest moment of his life. He was dizzy. His skin itched. Something fundamental had changed.

Was it his relative position in the world? Of course, he knew that the HEAVENLIES were worked on and improved in every possible way. That was part of the ten-year deal. But his mother was the first HEAVENLY he knew before and after, and he had never grasped the extent of the rejuvenation. In forty-some years, would he want to have the do-over himself, or perhaps pay to have it done sooner? Weren't there going to be any old-looking people any more? This had been going on for a long time, but he hadn't paid attention. For all he knew, he had hit on some over-eighty-five-year-old women who looked forty, and had gotten lucky. Jeez. Yuk.

That probably hadn't happened since the residents weren't allowed off the island, and until his mother arrived, he hadn't, thank God, gone over there.

"Say, Mother?"

"Yes, dear?"

"The Prolocutor omniplussed me the other day and asked if I'd be willing to bring my show here."

"What show?"

"I'm sure I must have told you about it. Anyway, I have a band. We entertain every weekend at a café in town."

"You never mentioned it."

"Well now you know." He hesitated. "It'll probably be a while till we come here to play but when we do—do me a favor—please don't tell anyone in the band you're my mother. Looking the way you do now—it might confuse them."

"Better they be confused than think I'm your date."
Huxley let that pass. She was right.

Tessa arrived early for the anniversary celebration. She spread out her blanket and set her collapsible bag on top. Inside was a bag of macadamias, Roy's favorite, a bag of pistachios, her favorite, seaweed cookies, napkins and two bubble-glasses. She leaned back on her elbows and stretched out her long legs, her face to the sun and the river.

Five minutes later, Wilbur came up and settled beside her. He was impossible to see in the grass, but Tessa knew he was there when she heard his music. She decided not to let Wilbur ruin things, even though it made her mad that Roy had brought him when she had asked him not to.

"Hey, Tessa," Roy said behind her. "You're a pretty sight."

"Thanks," Tessa said, sitting up to turn and smile.

"What you got in that bag?"

"Something to go with that nice, cold intoxofloat you're holding." Tessa elongated each word, Southern-style.

"Sounds good," Roy said. "Let's have a look."

Tessa stood, opened the bag and removed the bubble-glasses. "I'm real thirsty," she said and walked over to stand in front of him waiting for a kiss.

"Mmm. I wouldn't mind trying a few macadamias first." Roy reached down, grabbed half a handful and tossed them in his mouth. "Yum," he said. "Might try a few more." Another handful. Then he pulled the intoxofloat bottle out from under his arm, unwound and lifted the heavy wire holding down the cork. There was a pop and the fizzing drink burst out, geyser-like and streamed down over Tessa's hair, face and shoulders.

"Oh," she said, "shit."

"Sorry," Roy said, "I should have opened it in the other direction. Christ, you look like a drowned Siamese."

"Thanks, sweetheart," Tessa said, narrowing her eyes.

"I didn't mean anything."

"Don't you know this cat has claws? She might scratch if you don't say sorry."

"Of course I'm sorry, and I said so. Didn't you hear me?"

"I'm teasing. Come on, think of a toast."

"Okay," Roy said as he poured intoxofloat into her glass, then his. "How about...?"

"Wait, I've got it." She raised her glass. "To our future."

"Perfect. To our future." They clicked glasses and kissed.

"Mmm," Tessa said. "That was nice, but not exactly what I had in mind."

"Tessa." Roy looked serious.

"What's the matter? There's nobody around to watch and we're hidden by the bushes."

"We've got to talk."

"Well, I know that, but you could show a little affection. It's our anniversary and I want us to at least be in each other's arms when I tell you something."

"What?" Roy asked.

"Put your arms around me."

"Okay," Roy said, complying.

"I'm going to have a baby."

Roy pushed her away. "Come on, Tessa, that isn't possible. You said you've been protected the entire time we were together." He turned her around twice. "I don't see anything."

"Do you want to read the report?"

"No, damn it. I don't. And if you are pregnant, then do something about it. I'm not ready to be a father."

"But we talked about children and other things— marriage, for one."

"If we did, it was purely hypothetical and I was probably drunk."

"No, you weren't."

"Tessa, I'm not going to be involved."

"Well it's too late for that! Besides, everyone will know it's yours and, of course, it'll be a snap to prove."

"Well, I didn't sign the parenting papers, did I? You bitch, now I see the whole thing. You set me up, God damn you to hell!"

Roy tossed his half-full glass on the grass and began to stomp off.

Tessa ran up behind him, jumped on his back and wrapped her arms around his neck.

"I could break this," she said.

Roy quickly bent down and flipped her over his head. "Well, you weren't fast enough, Tessa," he said. "Good God, what a joke. Who could imagine you as a mother?" He looked down at her lying on the path, her legs spread, skirt up.

"I hate you," Tessa said.

"That's okay. I'm not real fond of you either."

Wilbur's music was playing, but neither Roy nor Tessa heard a note.

Melody was waiting for Sarah when she came out of the Memory. They had an appointment to discuss the upcoming Celebration.

"I'm sorry I'm late," Sarah said. "I lost track of time."

"What happened to you?' Melody asked. "You're wet and shivering."

"Come talk to me while I take a hot turbo," Sarah said. "I found out something I can't handle."

"Okay," Melody said. "But Ben's here, too. He has a message for you from Lionel.

"No problem," Ben called, who could pick up on conversations from afar. "I'll just play hide and seek with Babe. Oowee," he called softly from under the foundation planting next to the house.

Sarah opened the door for Babe to go out while Melody went into the bathroom and turned on the water.

"That's terrible," Melody said once Sarah, soaking and more relaxed, recounted in detail what had happened. "No wonder you're upset!"

"Yes. But it's ridiculous isn't it? I mean that happened a long time ago. It really shouldn't make a difference now."

"But it does," Melody said. "You'll never think of Jeff again without thinking of Tessa."

"It's hard to believe she did the same thing to both of us," Sarah said

"Except Roy wasn't my husband so it wasn't nearly as bad for me."

"But you loved him," Sarah said. "I think you hurt just as much as I do—maybe more because you're so young."

"Maybe." Melody said.

"It's a good thing I'll never have to see her again," Sarah said. "I just might punch her in the nose.

"That'll be the day," Melody said.

Sarah often strolled to the fishing dock while Babe played with Ben or Melody or slept on the porch. It was about a quarter of a mile from her house. She liked to throw stones in the water, one by one, and watch the circles intersect, then float away. She usually brought a book, sat on the slatted wood with her back against a post, knees up, and read until her bottom ached. That didn't take long; she no longer had much meat to sit on and always forgot to bring a cushion.

No one ever showed up on the afternoons she was there. It was reputed to be a meeting place at night for lovers, mostly employees of Pine Haven, she supposed, although when she headed there around four o'clock Sunday after the Memory fiasco, she realized that Jeff and Tessa might have met there a time or two before and during their affair. She nearly turned back when she heard a man's voice, loud, coming from nearby, but then there was silence, so she continued. She coughed several times and sneezed. She was definitely coming down with a cold.

She walked out on the dock, her book in hand, without noticing Tessa sitting cross-legged in the shadow of the hut.

"What the hell are you doing here?" Tessa demanded.

Sarah jumped. "Good Lord, you scared me nearly to death."

"Isn't that just a sweet shame?" Tessa said her lip curling.

"Sorry to disturb you," said Sarah. "I had no idea anyone was here."

"Finders keepers, right?"

"I guess," Sarah agreed, trying not to wonder if she was referring to Jeff as well as the location. "Well, so long."

"That's what I say—so long. It's been so long since Jeff died—the only man I ever truly loved."

"What's the point of…?"

"The point is I want to tell you how I feel. The point is you should know what a spoiled life you led, supported by that wonderful man. You didn't deserve him."

"I think you've had too much to drink, Tessa. Let's talk sometime when you're sober."

"I haven't been drunk in years. It feels great. You should try it, but then you're too perfect, aren't you?"

"Hardly."

"He thought so."

"Well, that's nice to know. Thank you."

"Do you have any idea how much I hate you?"

"Just because I was married to Jeff?"

"Yes. Isn't that enough?"

"I should be the one who hates you."

"You should, but you're too perfect."

"Come on, Tessa. I don't like this. I'm leaving."

"It would be real easy for me to push you into the river."

"Why would you want to do that?"

"So I could jump in and hold your head under water."

"You're crazy. I'm leaving. Please Tessa—let me by."

"No way."

Tessa folded her arms, body-blocked Sarah, then moved in as close as a lover, knocked the book from under her arm and kicked it so hard it flew off the dock. Then she shoved her again and again. Sarah tried to stand her ground but Tessa was bigger, stronger, younger and crazy drunk. When they neared the end of the dock, Tessa leaned over and head-butted Sarah in her stomach. Sarah fell, her shoulder hitting the dock hard. One arm hung over the edge, its hand nearly touching the water.

"Please, Tessa," she said. "Please stop."

Tessa stumbled to Sarah's side on the narrow dock. "You can go to hell, you old bitch." With a mighty shove she sent Sarah off the front of the dock and into the water.

As Sarah fell in, Tessa reeled backward, her arms windmilling. For a second she regained her balance, but lost it, regained it again, lost it and went over the side landing on her back on a patch of beach. The river was low and streamed over her legs while her upper body was on the sand. Tessa lay not moving; she had hit her head on some rocks. Beyond her lay *The Brothers Karamazov*, its blue binding half-buried in pebbles and sand.

It was never clear to Sarah how she'd managed to climb the dock steps, stand and walk away. She'd heard Tessa's splash and thump but thought at any moment that Tessa would reappear, push her into the river and drown her. She didn't notice or feel her sore, bleeding arms and legs, her bruised shoulder and side, her whole body shaking with cold. She didn't remember the book.

Run, she told herself. *Run*. But as in dreams when she was often stuck, nearly unable to move, she walked as if still in water, seeing the image of Tessa in close pursuit and feeling somehow under observation.

At his post outside the hospital, Ben noticed someone who looked to be the same height as Lionel and with a gait reminiscent of Lionel's circling around the building and exiting, head down, by the door in the west part of the fence around four o'clock. Of course, he knew it couldn't be Lionel—Lionel was in bed recuperating. Still, the more he thought of the resemblance, the more he wondered, and so he took off from the west gate, hoping he would run across whoever it was. Ben turned on the distance sensors of his recording system. He turned it down somewhat when he heard a woman shouting.

"Yes, you goddamn son of a bitch," shouted a drunken female voice north of where Ben stood. "You promised me the moon then flew off with what's-her-name."

"I didn't promise you the moon or anything else."

Doesn't sound like Lionel, Ben thought.

"Without a word," Tessa continued.

"I'm sorry, Tess, but I thought you understood me. We're both the same type, not to be taken seriously. Fun and games."

Tessa groaned.

"And that was months ago."

"Well, I haven't recovered," Tessa said.

"Sure you have," the man said. "Come off it.! What about Roy?"

"Him? He left just this minute—didn't you see him? Telling me it was all over and after only three months? Can you believe it? What a shit. All men are shits. Wait a minute. What's that?"

"Music," the man said. "Coming from the grass."

"It's Wilbur," Tessa said. "Roy forgot his best buddy. Ha."

"What?"

"That means he'll be back. Sooner rather than later. Say, can I ask you a favor?"

"What?"

"Would you bring him to me? All you need to do is follow the music."

"After the names you called me you want me to do you a favor?" the man said. "Oh, what the hell..."

Except for Tessa's heavy breathing, there was silence then music.

"I take it this is Wilbur."

"Yes."

"Here, catch." the man said.

"Thanks," Tessa said.

"Funny. Your ex-boyfriend seems like a nice guy."

"That's what I thought," Tessa said. "I thought we had something real."

"I'm sorry it didn't work out," the man said.

"Oh, sure. You really care—ha."

77

"Why so tough and mean.?

"He'll be sorry, and so will you and lots of people."

"Stop the blackmail shtick, Tessa. It's so old."

"I've got stuff on everyone. Things the authorities would love to know."

"Cut it out, Tessa. You're full of it."

"The police and such."

"Real glad I ran into you, Tessa. Real glad I could do you a favor."

"It'll probably be the last time."

"Why? Are you going back to the mountains?" Ben heard the man ask.

"No, I'm checking out."

The man paused. "You're taking this Roy business too seriously. He's obviously a bum."

"It takes one to know one."

"Well, you've got a good job and a good life. Think it over before you go."

"Never mind." She groaned again. "The hell with you."

"You better get home before you fall off the dock. You're drunk as a snake."

"Maybe so—but not as drunk as I'm going to be."

"You know what, Tessa? Oh the hell with it. I'm…"

Ben imagined the man shrugging as he turned and walked away mid-sentence. He continued to listen closely but didn't hear another word. Ben moved deeper into the woods and waited to see if the man he heard with Tessa would pass by.

Roy hadn't walked for long when he realized he'd forgotten Wilbur. Jesus, he'd have to go back, which meant he'd have to see and talk to Tessa again. What the fuck could he say to her? Maybe think of a way to sweet-talk her into losing the baby. He could tell her it just wasn't the right time, that they'd have one in a couple of years. He'd apologize and make love to her. What the hell. It wasn't going to kill him.

But when he arrived at the dock, Sarah was there as well and he stood in the bushes beside the boathouse and watched the entire scene between her and Tessa. He was about to rescue Sarah and was standing on the side of the dock when she climbed up the ladder and limped by without seeming to see him. "Are you all right?" he asked. No answer. He watched as she slowly disappeared beyond the trees. Then he looked for Wilbur near where Tessa had been sitting before Sarah arrived. He wasn't there and the device to alert him didn't work, and Roy didn't hear any music. Something was wrong. Then he moved quickly from the shore over the sodden sand and sloshed down to where Tessa lay.

She'd taken quite a fall. Maybe she had broken her neck. Maybe she was dead. Terrible to think it, but that would be a piece of luck. The water covered half of Tessa's body—her head rested on the sand. Roy knelt in the water and studied her closely. She wasn't his idea of the mother of his children but, God, was she something to look at, a natural beauty. What a shame it had turned out this way.

Instinctively, he reached under her head, and found a bed of rocks. Sharp ones. She wasn't moving but when he put his finger on her throat, he felt a pulse. She was alive. Unconscious, but alive. He washed her blood off his hands and was thinking of what to do when Tessa opened her eyes. Christ, she was looking straight at him.

"You bastard," she whispered. "Help me."

"Where's Wilbur?" Roy demanded.

"Riv-ver."

He barely understood her. She made a choking sound. *Was she laughing?*

"Tossed him." She made the sound again.

Yes, she was laughing. He felt the blood rush to his head.

"Help me," Tessa said again.

"Sure thing, sweetheart," Roy said, deciding what to do as he said it. *The bitch had destroyed Wilbur.* He raised Tessa's head gently and slammed it against the rocks, once, twice and again. He waited. Her eyes were open and fixed. There was no pulse. He felt sick and out of breath. He'd never killed anyone before. Of course, she had been almost dead and if he hadn't found her, she might have drowned in the rising water. *Shit, that would have been perfect. Why was I so goddamn impulsive? Shit.*

Now he had to look for Wilbur's remains and get away without being seen. Anyone could walk by. He splashed up and down both sides of the dock searching, head down. Then he stomped onto the dock to get what he thought might be a better view. No way could he see parts of a tiny green crocodile. He'd have to return when the river was nearly dry. Then, as he walked back on the dock looking from side to side, he saw a glint of something in the water to his left, caught by the western sun splayed through the pines across the river. It was Wilbur—what had been Wilbur.

"That bitch!" He waded into the river and picked up the little robot pieces and put them in his pocket. Then he took a discreet path inside the woods where he and Tessa had walked a time or two while he was still seeing Melody. It curved toward, then away from the hospital and back to employee quarters. He didn't see anyone.

Ben had stopped the audio, reviewed the recording of the conversation and wondered why Tessa had said, "I'm checking out," instead of "I'm quitting," or "I'm leaving." Much later, he discovered when he looked it up, that unless you were in a hotel, it could mean about to die. Too bad he hadn't understood it at the time. Tessa might have been contemplating suicide, and saying those words was her call for help. Had the man heard that as a possibility? If so, he ignored it.

Ben began walking toward the fishing dock. His sensors told him there was someone on the path. He slid quietly into the woods to hide and watch. Lionel appeared. It hadn't sounded like him on audio but there he was.

Lionel must have been the man he'd heard arguing with Tessa and so it must have been Lionel sidling out of the hospital earlier.

He continued on the woods path to the dock. There was absolute silence on the audio. At least he knew where Tessa was and that she couldn't get far in her inebriated condition. Once he found her, he would escort her home. It was part of his job to protect everyone, residents first, guests second and employees last. If she were too hard to handle, he'd signal for assistance. Later, Ben realized he should have done that right then, or earlier, because by the time he reached the dock, Tessa was lying dead on her back in the clear, sandy-bottomed, rock-filled river, eyes wide open as if in surprise.

Ben was correct. Lionel had left the hospital Sunday afternoon around four o'clock after worrying for hours that someone would steal his costume, especially the bloodstained beard, eyebrows and wig, as a memento. He was, after all, a Living Treasure and former senator, and you never knew what people would consider a prize.

Zack was snoring, head slumped to the side, looking oddly comfortable in the hospital chair when Lionel had eased out of bed, and removed from his closet the grungy underwear, pants, shirt, socks and boots from the night before, put them on with distaste, and rolled up everything else inside his jacket. Then he slipped out into the hall, chin buried in his collection, to leave unnoticed by way of the stairs and a supply door he found in the basement. When he got home, he showered and changed into clean clothes to wear the next day when he was scheduled for release. He was back in the hospital, feeling great, less than thirty minutes from when he'd left, and except for a man, dripping wet from the knees down, he hadn't seen a soul. Zack had stopped snoring and was fast asleep when he crept back into bed. No sweat.

Late Sunday afternoon, Sarah omniplussed Ben on his resident receiver. He was still outside the hospital, even though Zack had come out to tell him Lionel was fine and could probably go home the next day.

"Ben," she said. "Can you come over right away?"

"What's the matter?" asked Ben.

"I'd like you to watch Babe for a little while. I left a message with Melody to take her home when she gets back. I have a terrible cold. Can you hear it?"

"Yes."

"I just hope it's not turning into pneumonia. At my age, you never know."

The old person's friend, Ben thought. "I've already signaled the Medivan. We're both on our way."

"That's wonderful," Sarah said. "Thanks."

She was waiting for him, a small satchel by her side and Babe on her lap, in an heirloom iron chair outside the house. Babe leaped off when she saw Ben and jumped on his back with a joyful yip.

Sarah was wearing a coat that covered her arms, legs and neck. She was shaking and looked gray.

"I was in the ocean earlier today," she explained. "Caught my death."

"The ocean?" Ben said. "It's way too rough for people to swim today. Didn't you hear my report and prediction?"

"Right," Sarah said. "I wasn't thinking."

She wouldn't mention it to anyone else. It didn't make sense. She'd have to explain and she couldn't. They'd understand about the Memory, but not about her trip half a mile into the ocean. It wasn't part of Jeff's documented Celebration. And she didn't understand how she could catch a cold today from a dip taken over two years ago during it, although it was probably what happened later at the dock that had really made her sick.

Sarah decided she wasn't going to say another thing, especially not about what Tessa had tried to do. Tessa was so drunk she probably wouldn't remember any of it and would deny everything, and there was a very good chance people would believe her. Tessa was not only self-confident and convincing, she was one of the most popular employees at Pine Haven—everyone would assume it was Sarah who was either lying or nuts.

"Okay with you if Babe and I try to find Melody?" Ben asked. "She may be in the hospital visiting Lionel."

"I didn't know Melody knew him that well." Sarah frowned.

"Don't ask me," Ben said, "but she was with him before he collapsed early this morning."

Ben left out the details that would have made that bit of information less provocative.

Melody never said anything about sleeping with Lionel—but then why would she? It was none of my business, thought Sarah. *Men and fornication. You'd think I'd be used to it by now. Well, serves the old coot right.*

"What floor's he on?"

"Don't know but I'll get back to you when I do."

"Thanks. I need to ask him if he'd be willing to adopt Babe a little earlier than planned. Zack said Lionel was in good shape and might be released tomorrow."

"I didn't know you knew Zack," Ben said.

"Lionel asked him to ask me for a rain-check," Sarah said. "He'd made a date to take Babe flying this morning."

Damn that Lionel! she thought. *If he hadn't collapsed from screwing too much, she wouldn't have entered the Memory late, and so the whole time with Jeff would have been different, or rather, the same as it had always been. No swim in the sea, no Tessa, no rotten cold.*

Two of Ben's friends were now in the hospital, same floor, with similar views if either looked out. Sarah was in and out of sleep, semi delirious, and running a temperature of one hundred and four point five. "She may not make it," the nurse confided to Zack, who was standing by under orders from Lionel. "She should have come in earlier. Ben says she was fine this morning," Zack said.

The doctors of Pine Haven treated patients as if they would return, when cured, to lives of great expectations—even those scheduled soon for Departure. What a joke, Sarah would have said if she had been awake and in her right mind. Lionel, alone in his room and alert as never before, or so he thought, was making a mental list.

- start book re life
- no, hate to write--have no talent
- hire ghostwriter
- no, wouldn't like telling someone else my business
- record life on insta-mem
- no, don't know how to use insta-mem – hate contraptions except airplanes
- get someone to show me
- ask Zack.
- start immediately
- be honest even if it kills me

The insta-mem thought-retriever turned out to be easy. It only took Zack a few minutes to show him how it worked so that later, if he so desired, he could listen to the sound of his own voice and delight in the cadences of his own sentences.

"My life," Lionel began, "just the high points. I don't want to bore anyone with my birth, childhood or elections to office. Facts like that are available to anyone curious enough to check them out. This is about what went on behind the scenes. Things no one knows, that I never wanted anyone to know, and maybe this will be for my ears only. I haven't decided because it depends on how it turns out. It may be more shameful than I expect and I may have to leave a few things out to protect the innocent, as they say, although, not counting my sons, I doubt there are any innocents in my story, except my first wife, Louella.

"Sweet! And way too young to be mixed up with a fellow like me. I mean, I was bad news—used to get drunk, hang out with losers, the usual profile for an idiot alpha male—and although not old enough to be her father, sometimes I felt like I was—old enough, I mean. I wasn't near good enough for her, but neither of us knew that—we were too dumb and too full of lust and love. We were crazy about each other—I couldn't keep my hands off of her.

"Hard to believe now that I'm old and cold, but it was true as blue then and, of course, the inevitable happened. Did I use condoms? Damn right, but don't you know—God knows I didn't—those stupid things weren't one hundred percent. Of course, we got married, not because of her father or mother saying we had to or else, but because I knew it was right.

"She wasn't even sixteen and, shit forever, before she reached her seventh month she miscarried and died. Don't ask me why. I couldn't understand what the doctor said—I was too out of my mind. If we'd been near a better hospital, maybe it would've been different. I couldn't believe she was gone except she turned so blue and before a minute passed, she was as cold as the grave. I ask myself if I still feel guilty and I guess I don't. Time does change things and it was so long ago.

"At the time, though, I felt as bad as I'm capable of feeling, guilty and grief-stricken, and sick in my heart and stomach. I couldn't forgive myself and her mother told me she never wanted to see my face again, even though we lived in the same town. I was twenty-five and didn't feel like such a big shot anymore. I told my daddy if the offer was still good, I'd go to any college I could get into and learn to be something—I didn't care what.

"My daddy said as long as the school was below the Mason-Dixon line, he'd be happy. And there was one more thing. 'I'm not paying for you to become a lawyer,' he said. "I don't like lawyers.'

'You don't study law in college, Daddy,' I said. 'You got to go to law school for that.'

Of course, by the time I finished college, my daddy was gone and I had more than enough of his money to pay my own way through the University of South Carolina Law School. I don't believe I'd have even thought of it if my daddy hadn't put the idea in my head."

When Zack started for home Sunday night, it was nearly midnight. Except for nodding off in the hospital chair, he hadn't slept for forty-eight hours. He was exhausted, but the adrenalin still stirred. The nurse had kicked him out of Sarah's room at ten-thirty. Zack was afraid she'd feel his absence and something bad would happen. Sarah's temperature hadn't budged. She was listed as critical.

He was glad to find Ben outside, eager for a chat as always.

"Quite a day," Zack said.

"I'll say." Ben looked up at him with sympathy.

"I'm pooped."

"You should be," Ben said. "You weren't designed to stay awake for two days."

"Maybe a genius will figure out how to make that possible."

"Half-man, half-robot?" Ben asked.

"Something like that."

"Then we'd be related," Ben said.

"Don't hold your breath," Zack said.

"Say, did Lionel stay in his room all afternoon?"

"I was asleep most of the time, but I assume so," Zack said. "Where else would he have been?"

"Don't know. Just curious."

As soon as Zack opened his door, the voice message was triggered and he heard Annemarie's honeyed vowels.

"Hey there, Zack, sweetie. Do you know who this is?" She paused as if to give him time to respond.

"It's me, Annemarie. Last night you said you were going to get in touch right away? Well, I waited and waited all day and now it's ten o'clock at night. Where are you, handsome? Omniplus me. I'll be up for a while." She left her reach and made a smooching noise.

Damn, he thought. *What was he going to say when he omniplussed her back? He'd have to ask the senator. Lionel probably loved to give advice about this sort of thing.*

MONDAY, AUGUST 14, 2073

"No advice," Lionel said firmly, the next morning after his release from the hospital. "Not anymore. I'm not getting involved in your love life again. It's too dangerous. Look what happened Saturday night."

"You won't have to get involved," Zack hastily assured him. "Just tell me how to get rid of her in a nice way."

"Tell her you're dying. You've got a communicable terminal disease."

"Come on."

"Why do you want to get rid of her? She's a terrific girl."

"How do you know?"

Lionel struck his thigh. "Damn it all. Hell, who cares? You'd find out sooner or later." He looked up as if there were something stuck on the ceiling. "I used to see her."

"You mean you went out with her?"

"Uh huh."

"Spent the night with her?" Zack sounded triumphant.

"Zack, come on. That's enough."

"Thanks, you've answered my question."

"Huh?"

"She's your girl, or was."

"So what?"

"I have a rule."

"What is it?"

"Never date a friend's ex."

Zack wondered if there were any girls the senator didn't know well enough to say, she's terrific, or she's not so great. *At least,* he thought, *Melody isn't one of them.* Not that he thought she was pure; he just hoped she was pretty pure because although he wasn't a virgin, he respected abstinence, especially in women.

Another one of his rules was to refrain from sex most of the time, meaning he seldom went out with women. However, he was willing to forget his principles for Melody. He believed she liked him deep down, but just didn't know it yet. When you care for someone that much, it had to be reciprocal. Maybe if he wrote her a letter, she would wake up to his abiding passion. Yes, a letter was the perfect idea. He decided to do it before he could think about it any longer.

"Senator, could I trouble you for a piece of paper and an envelope?"

"Happy to. Let me see what I can find." Lionel opened a drawer and took out a box. This should do, plain, no initials. Do you need a pen too?"

"That would be a big help," Zack said.

Lionel handed him one. The ink had a metallic quality to it, sort of a deep gray.

"Thanks," said Zack. "Do you mind if I sit at the table on your terrace?"

He didn't bother waiting to hear a reply. He was a man with a purpose.

He wrote in the architect's print he'd practiced for years, but rarely used.

Dear Melody,

I'm not good at writing letters and I've never written a poem before, but here goes.

Bluer than summer skies,
The stars don't shine as bright as your eyes.
The day you wear some gold with black,
I'll fly you to the moon and back.
This is just to let you know you mean the world to me.

Always and forever,
Puzzle Lover.

Zack reread his poem with satisfaction. Not half bad, he thought. He put the letter in Lionel's envelope and wrote Miss Melody on top. He'd take it to her door and slip it under while she was at work. He had to join her there in a little while, so there was no possibility she'd catch him in the act.

He handed the box of stationery and the pen back to Lionel. "Thanks, Senator," he said.

Lionel waved, watched Zack disappear over a dune, and then watched as Ben, too, disappeared.

Ben followed Zack to Melody's apartment, saw him slip something under her door, then take off. He followed Zack to the Departure Pavilion, and then Ben contacted the hospital. Sarah was a bit better, temperature down to one hundred and three. Ben was relieved. His friends were accounted for, and all signs indicated that Sarah was on the mend.

Lionel settled down to listen to more of his life on disk. "Come here, Babe," he called. "Bone, here's your bone." Babe jumped onto his lap.

His voice filled the room. "As it turned out, it wasn't so hard to become a lawyer. I wasn't at the top of my class, didn't make Law Review, but I had friends who were and did and that was almost as good, maybe better, because throughout my life, those fellows never let me down. I never let them down either, especially once they helped me get into the House and later, the Senate, where I could help them in significant ways.

"They were smarter than me, but I was bigger and better-looking, and had a way of talking that people cottoned to. It came natural—my daddy was the same. He could have been a politician if he'd wanted, but he loved the small town life and wouldn't leave it for the world until the accident, when he had no choice. None of us could ever figure out what happened. He'd handled a surfboard since he was old enough to stand. Mama never got over it. Died before her time. But she did get to know my second wife, Olivia. Didn't like her much, but enjoyed the twins Olivia bore me, her only grandchildren, as it turned out.

"Olivia was as sour as Louella had been sweet. I guess I thought I loved her or why would I have married her? She wasn't even pregnant until a year or so after the wedding. After she swelled up with Bob and Billy, I lost all interest in her. Except for her enormous belly, the rest of her was scrawny, her skin had spots and she had a pickled smell no matter what perfume she used. And by her seventh month there was a four-inch red slash that started above her belly button and went down nearly to her bush. Later, it turned into a white and wrinkly scar. You'd think she'd been cut open in battle, and Olivia sometimes said she had.

"It's not proper to talk ill or make fun of the dead, which is what Olivia is and has been for sixty years. She died of unnatural causes, according to the police. I can't remember much about the evening except we'd been fighting and drinking—nothing unnatural about that— and she slipped and fell on the marble floor, polished to a fare-thee-well, in the front hall. Hit her pretty birdlike head and that was that. So, I was left a widower again, but this time with two children to look after. I guess a few people in town thought I was responsible for Bob and Billy's mother's untimely passing, but I've never paid much attention to what people think or say.

"That brings me to Pamela, my third and last wife. Every man's got to have a wind-up and mine was a doozy. Pretty, smart, athletic and crazy about my boys—the perfect stepmother. She wanted to have a bunch of kids of our own. Never happened and she didn't want to adopt. What does a person named Pamela look like? Would you say tall, blond, fair? That's what I'd say, but we'd both be wrong. She was tall, all right, but her hair and skin were dark—the blackest Irish mixed with Mexican. I truly loved her, though I guess at the end, she didn't believe it.

"The problem was, I'd gotten in the habit of fooling around, and it was so easy and seemed so harmless, I didn't give it up. I should have, of course, but in those years I was puffed up with my own importance and the ladies always go for the power boys, especially if they aren't too bad to look at and, as I've already said, I wasn't. I'm not bothering to be modest here. What's the point? From the perspective of a man over one hundred, I behaved like an idiot. Nothing I can do about it now except admit the fact. I guess that's better than some would do.

"In a town like Washington—I was a senator by then—you can get away with murder, but along about the tenth victim, someone's going to talk. Once Pamela realized what a piece of shit her husband was she was in a depression nearly non-stop. Of course at that point I didn't know she was on to me but with Pammy's go-ahead I went to see her shrink, and he told me my philandering was the reason for her mental state. Somehow I believed we could resuscitate our marriage and that from then on we were doing great. I didn't sleep with anyone but her after that, and tried to make it up to her in other ways.

"About six months after her doctor let me know he thought I was dirt, Pammy committed suicide following a depression so deep no pill could pull her out. Her note read, 'Sorry, honey, not your fault. Glory, glory, how I used to love you, Pammy.' The policeman said it was the goddamn nicest suicide note he'd ever read.

"I didn't see it coming. I should have sued the idiot doctor for not hospitalizing her, but to tell the truth, I didn't have the strength. At age fifty-six, I was 0 for 3 and I wasn't getting into the game again.

"It's not so easy to talk about my sons, Bob and Billy. They were good boys who went to the best schools, had nice friends, bright futures and then got caught up in one of the string of nasty wars we were always waging around the world in the thirties about where displaced persons from drowned islands and flooded low lying countries should go since there was less and less land and more and more people requiring resettlement. Everyone over eighteen had to serve unless there was a medical reason. Bob lost a leg and Billy was killed. Instantaneous. A smartwave hit his saferocket. Took me years to handle it, the same as after Louella died. Bob's doing fine, became a lawyer. I was flattered, and he's a grandpa himself. In ten years, he'll be eligible for HEAVEN unless the government raises the age requirement again. I wouldn't be surprised.

"They sent Billy's body home, of course. I visit his grave once a month. Sometimes I pray—it seems the right thing to do—but to whom? I'm not a believer. Just the same, I talk to Billy, tell him what's going on. Bob told me he saw him after he died and I didn't ask for details. Twins have a special relationship and I didn't want to tell Bob that was why he was imagining things. One good thing was that Bob and I felt okay about the loss of his leg because, by God, he was alive. What else mattered? The therapy and prosthetic were effective and in what seemed like no time, he was running his miles every morning and playing tennis as before.

"After the boys came home, one in a box, I lost myself in flying lessons and bought myself a little silver Jupitour jet. I used it during my next campaign and flew all over the state, and later when I was a candidate for president, all over the country. I had the time of my life, met and bedded more beautiful women than ought to have been legal. I was photographed and talked about as if I were a fucking celebrity. It wasn't just because I was a presidential candidate—it was because of my silver jet, silver hair and the gorgeous girls I took out to dinner. People loved to read about me, but they didn't elect me the fifty-fourth President of the United States. Just as well. Except for my looks, I wasn't Mount Rushmore material."

Delirium behind her, pneumonia at bay, Sarah omniplussed Clarissa.

Before she could speak, Clarissa said, "I can't believe you're calling. Barkley and I are on our way."

"To make plans?"

"No, to be with you. The doctor said you were—uh—dying."

"Well I'm not. I'm fine or almost. Amazing what tricks the medicine men have up their sleeves these days."

"Well, you're certainly in no condition to travel," Clarissa said.

"I will be in a couple of days and I want to make plans."

"We'll talk when the doctors send you home."

"You mean you're not coming after all?"

"No, mother. What's the point now?"

None, she supposed. The doctors wouldn't release her right away, and she already knew her children weren't going to be helpful in her flight to life. She needed someone she could count on and at this point the only person she could think of was Lionel.

To her surprise, the 'How To' book had helped. So simple. She reversed her tracks from a hide-away in New England back to a car, back to a private plane, back to a boat, back to a swim in the ocean where, if all went well, the Administration would believe she had drowned.

Ben, in his innocence, could help her figure out the best, that is to say the worst time for her to go for the swim from which she would never return. Lionel would pick her up in the ocean, take her to land, and then to his plane. Everything depended on him.

She'd have to have access to money to sustain her for the rest of her life, and Lionel could sell her stash of diamonds, her rainy day security, one at a time as needed for cash—no eyebrows raised. It would work; it made sense.

Sarah was certain a man of his position and wealth could figure out how to make it all happen—no problem. Lionel had made it clear he considered her a friend, said he would miss her, and had already taken in her beloved dog. It followed he'd be willing to help her.

She'd have to explain she wasn't going to cheat HEAVEN. Not really. Her disappearance wasn't going to cost the government another dime. She would merely be depriving them of her body. When she was free, she would claim her age was forty-eight so there'd be no question of asking for government assistance; she would pay for everything herself.

Lionel would have to provide her with ID just in case she needed it. Eventually, she would die on her own, nobody the wiser.

She pictured herself ensconced in a small, bleached gray, weather-beaten cottage with gray-blue shutters somewhere north, near the ocean in walking distance to a town. She expected she might not be as healthy when separated from the total ministrations of Pine Haven so she'd hire some pleasant young man or woman to purchase and deliver her qwik-chow and fruit as well as assist her as necessary. The local doctor would take care of any sprained ankles or colds. No hospital stays. She'd refuse to go no matter what ailed her.

Any day past August twenty-eighth was borrowed time, so she'd be ready whenever the Reaper arrived, even if it was the day after. She'd have a big smile on her face, if she had the sense to recognize him.

Every few years, a bill was introduced in Congress to ensure that all HEAVENLIES had a tracking chip inserted in their upper arms. Those in favor argued it would be for the residents' own protection in case they wandered off; they denied it was to prevent HEAVENLIES from changing their minds and finding a way to escape. Human rights groups always spoke up for the residents. "It's an assault on privacy," they clamored. *Thank God,* thought Sarah. If it had been passed, she wouldn't have a prayer.

Melody didn't know what to make of the note. Was Lionel the puzzle lover? She suspected so, but then why did he write Miss Melody on the envelope? Huxley was the only one who called her that. Maybe Lionel had heard Huxley call her Miss Melody during the show. Also, it didn't sound like anything Huxley would write. He could write verse easily. Maybe he was being funny in his sarcastic way. That made some sense, but no, not possible. Huxley didn't even know where she lived. Must be Lionel. He mentions flying. Who else could it be? Zack? No, he was like a brother or a cousin, a sweet, shy cousin. He was attractive; they all were, in different ways. Maybe it was someone she hardly knew. She was getting more and more excited.

The handwriting would clear it up. She needed samples. Also the ink was unusual, a metallic gray she'd never seen before. Later, she noticed that it shone in the dark. Weird. It was a cinch to check out Zack's handwriting. He kept a log at the Departure Pavilion. But she needed a glimpse of Lionel's. He might have signed something at the hospital before his operation. She had lots of connections at the hospital, so that should be simple.

Gold and black. Why gold and black? Because black rhymed with back. She understood the writer's dilemma. It could have been any color and black, but gold and black it was. A scarf would work. She had a black one with gold and green swirls. She'd nearly given it away. Sometimes it pays to hold onto things.

Tomorrow, she would scout out who Puzzle Lover was. Tonight she would swallow a meal pill and go to bed early at nine o'clock, note by her side.

Later, in bed when she closed her eyes, her grandmother's face appeared. Was she always watching and listening to her? It felt that way. It felt as if her grandmother knew everything and wanted to tell her to simmer down—that she was healthy and good-looking with a lovely voice. That should be enough. Well, it wasn't.

Granny, are you listening? What I truly want is fame and a little fortune—but mostly fame. Is that disgusting? I know you must think so. I also want some babies and a good man to be their father, who will want to help me and be good to us. I guess I want it all. Sometimes I can hardly sleep, picturing how wonderful it all would be.

Okay Granny, if you hear my thoughts, I have a question for you. Am I going to die young? Sometimes I feel like I am. I think about death a lot. Maybe it's because I'm around people in perfectly good health but near Departure. At the end I help them die and, finally, I check their bodies out of Pine Haven forever. I tell myself I don't mind—it's just a job—but I sort of do. Honestly, Granny, half the time I don't know what I think. Is that normal for someone my age? I've never asked any of my friends if they know or don't know what they think about things. Do you think death might be better than uncertainty? It would be so nice to be sure, to know your dreams are going to come true. Such a lot of crap, right?

Sarah will Depart two weeks from today. I care about her even though the Prolocutor warned against it. I can't help it. She comforted me when I was sick over Roy a while back, and we comforted each other yesterday. Funny how fast I got over Roy. Now I'm glad he glommed onto Tessa. She can have him, although there were a few hours when I could have killed them both.

Tessa was officially dead. Babe found her Monday evening when she, Ben and Zack went for a walk. Tessa was just under the water, face-up, her eyes wide open, in the narrow part of the river that bordered one side of the landing area. Babe caught her scent and barked until Zack came over.

Zack hadn't seen Tessa in a while but knew her well, as did all the residents on the island and many in Sywannah. There were rumors she had either slept with everyone at the Sex Clinic or in private. As he stared down at her, horrified, Zack realized that, even with her face beginning to bloat, she reminded him of Annemarie. The coloring, rather than the features, her hair, skin and eyes. *Especially the eyes*, he thought, seeing Tessa's face when alive in his mind's eye. They must be related somehow. No wonder Annemarie had looked familiar.

According to Investigator Krantz, Tessa had been dead for at least twenty-four hours. The coroner would be more exact as to the time and cause of death.

"You say the dog found her?" Krantz asked.

Zack nodded. Speech was nearly beyond him. He had omniplussed for help and then gone to look for Lionel whom he found sitting on his terrace in the midst of listening to another chapter of his life. Zack pointed toward the airfield and pulled Lionel's arm.

"Come," he said, nearly choking.

Lionel saw this was no time for questions, so he followed Zack in silence to the river.

"My God," Lionel said, kneeling on the bank and looking down at Tessa. "I can't believe this. I bumped into her on Saturday. She seemed happy. Said she was going to celebrate her three-month anniversary with her boyfriend."

Zack raised his eyebrows.

"His name's Roy something, Lionel said.

When Lionel repeated this to Investigator Krantz, he, too, wanted to know about Roy. "And," Krantz said, "I need a timeline for both of you." He tucked his notebook into his jacket pocket and grinned. "You used to go with her, didn't you, Senator? Maybe she was giving you a hard time."

"Huh?" Lionel said. "Shit. That was four years ago, for Chrissakes."

"Not very long ago in my book," Krantz said.

"We were just friends."

"Probably so. Still, a timeline, okay? And you, Mr. Dakota. Did you know the deceased?"

Zack nodded.

"Cat got your tongue?" Krantz asked.

"He's too upset to talk," Lionel explained. "It was a shock, finding Tessa. I think he'll be okay by tomorrow."

Zack nodded.

"Say, how's your fiancée?" asked the investigator.

Zack nodded again.

"I guess that means she's fine. Come to the station first thing tomorrow morning and we'll talk if you can by then. Bring your timeline. You too, Senator."

Lionel smiled and imagined the investigator pinned against the wall by the Chief of Police.

"We need your timeline, Frankie boy. You knew the lady pretty well, didn't you? Maybe she was going to tell the wife."

The Investigator gulped.

The Chief continued. "It certainly wouldn't surprise me if the perpetrator lived on our side of the bay."

Maybe I should write mysteries, thought Lionel, worried about how he'd spend his time once his and the Questar past was exhausted. Maybe he could solve this mystery, insta-mem it, then find another murder to solve, or invent a murder-mystery and insta-mem that. What a great idea.

Before Tessa's body was photographed and removed, and the crime scene—if that's what it was—was secured, Lionel and Zack returned to the house where Ben was watching Babe.

"I know you can't speak," Lionel told Zack. "So just write answers to my questions on this piece of paper." He handed his pen to Zack.

"Do you know Roy?" Lionel asked.

Zack wrote, 'Don't think so.'

"Yeah," Lionel said. "I'd have to see his picture to be sure. You run into so many people, it's hard to remember all their names."

Zack nodded.

"Did you like Tessa?"

'Sure,' Zack wrote. 'She was okay.'

"Did you have sex with her?"

'Come on,' Zack wrote. 'You wouldn't tell me.'

"This is different. Tessa's been murdered."

'Maybe there's another explanation,' Zack wrote.

"Oh, God," Lionel said.

Zack raised his eyebrows in a 'what's-the-matter' expression.

"I've got to omniplus Annemarie."

'Why?' Zack's eyebrows asked.

"She's Tessa's younger sister and next of kin. Damn it all, I should have told the investigator to do it." He pursed his lips and appraised Zack. "It just hit me—you said Annemarie's expecting you to omniplus. When do you suppose you'll get your voice back?"

'Not sure,' Zack wrote. 'Tomorrow?'

"That's too late," Lionel said. "She's got to hear about Tessa now before it's all over the wall-to-wall."

Lionel poured himself a gin and took a belt. "Okay, damn it all, I'll omniplus her." He punched in the code, sat down, his big head in his hands. "Hey there, where are you off to?" he asked Zack, who was inching toward the door. "I can see out of the top of my head." He pointed to a chair. "Stick around, my friend; I'm afraid I'm going to need you."

Annemarie's screams on the omniplus were repeated when Lionel and Zack flew over to the mainland to pick her up an hour later. She beat on Lionel's chest. "Was it you, you bastard? Love them and heave them?"

Zack carried her out with the bag she'd managed to pack before they arrived. She wouldn't let Lionel touch her. She was crying, but not hysterical.

"There, there," Zack said, as if she were a baby. "There, there." His voice had returned without him or Lionel noticing. Funny how easy it was for him to talk to Annemarie.

They flew from St. Miguel to Pine Haven as slowly as possible then circled for an hour with Annemarie slumped in the back seat. To their relief, she cried herself into a deep sleep.

"No," she said from inside her nightmare. "No."

"She hates me," Lionel said when they landed, "so she'd better stay with you."

"What about Tessa's place?"

"Forget that."

"You're right," Zack said, "but maybe Sarah wouldn't mind, or Melody."

"Sarah's still in the hospital and Melody's asleep by now. I don't think we've got a choice."

"Jesus," Zack said. "What will people think?" By people, he meant Melody.

"How old are you, Zack?" Lionel didn't wait for an answer. "Doesn't matter. You're old enough to have figured out that people don't care what the hell you do as long as you don't involve or inconvenience them."

Zack pondered a moment. *Bullshit,* he thought.

Lionel continued. "Unless you're married."

Annemarie stirred. Zack turned, reached back and patted her hand. "There, there," he said.

The more Ben learned about people, the more he saw similarities in himself, although he couldn't help but note that he carried everything to an extreme. He overdid loyalty and truthfulness to the detriment of sense and discretion. Once he realized this, he began to censor himself before speaking, though because distressing events were distracting his friends at present, they didn't notice the change. He found himself spending more time with Babe. It was a simpler relationship and, besides, they were both animals, even if Babe breathed and he didn't.

Ben was shocked to see Tessa's body because he hadn't considered the possibility she might float down the river from the fishing dock to where Babe discovered her near the airstrip. If he'd had the sense to consider the possibility—the events of the day before had muddled his braincomp—he would somehow have managed to lead Zack and Babe away from the landing area.

He hadn't wanted to be the one to report Tessa's death on the chance he'd be questioned, and might have to implicate someone he cared for. He knew that three of his good friends disliked Tessa. Lionel, who seemed fond of everyone, ex-girlfriends included, was one. And Ben had seen Lionel sneaking back to the hospital the afternoon Tessa died. Melody and Sarah were the others. He had overheard a conversation between them on Sunday, Sarah said Tessa had seduced Jeff, which ruined her recollection of their last days together, and Melody said Tessa had seduced Roy while she thought he still loved her.

Humans were too complicated. He didn't understand the seduction thing and he was beginning to wish he'd chosen another subject for his dissertation.

At six o'clock, Huxley stood at his newly installed vintage stove, sautéing octopus, garlic and shallots, while listening to the country music songs he would rehearse on Thursday, when the sound on the omniview wall of his apartment increased in volume, as it was set to do when there was local news. Tessa Posnoff's body had been found a half-hour earlier in Winding Creek. Anyone who saw Tessa on Sunday was asked to contact the local police department at once. She had been dead at least twenty-four hours. Foul play was suspected.

He turned off the flame, the music and news, and sat on the window seat overlooking Charles Street. He no longer felt like eating. Poor Tessa. He might have been the last person to see her, unless she was murdered, which he doubted. She must have fallen off the dock and drowned, especially as she had threatened to get even drunker after he left. There was still plenty of intoxofloat in the bottle and she was already reeling.

"It was my idea to meet Roy here for a little celebration," Tessa had told him. "This is where we got together the first time and we'd hardly been apart for three wonderful months."

"Wasn't it a little too soon to celebrate?" he'd asked.

"No, it was a little too late because not long after he opened the bottle he dumped me. Boom, like that."

Huxley had made a sympathetic sound. It had served to irritate the already angry Tessa.

It hit him he shouldn't have left her alone yesterday, but, hell, she wasn't his responsibility. He looked after himself and that was it. Period.

He expected he would hear from the police by morning. The to-and–from launch records would show he'd been on the island from one-thirty to four forty-five Sunday afternoon. They would find out his mother lived there— she was, after all, the only Soong on the island and it wasn't a common name. They would also find out there were two ways to get from her house to the launch and that one of them passed right by the fishing dock. If they didn't discover all of that right away, Huxley would still be questioned because many would remember that he and Tessa had been an item not so long ago.

He needed to go into the station though he didn't know yet what he would say. Clearly, it would be better to volunteer information rather than have it dragged out of him, but then no one had seen him near the dock and he could have walked to the launch the other way. If he told the police he'd seen Tessa and talked to her, how could he convince them he didn't kill her? It would be a mess.

He'd have to hire a lawyer; the story would be all over Swyannah. His gorgeous women clients would know he'd lied to them about his sexual orientation. His band would be kaput and worst of all, he might be found guilty and put in jail for something he didn't do. He'd been feeling sorry for Tessa, but now he was furious with her. The foolish behavior that led to her unnecessary death was about to ruin his life. He'd kill her if she were still alive.

Huxley warmed the octopus, added chopped dulse, slid it all from pan to plate, removed fresh socca from the warmer, dressed his wheatgrass salad, poured some verivino blanc into a chilled wine glass and sat down for dinner. He would hang tough.

Later that evening, Huxley, wine-confident, took the initiative and paid the police station a visit. Investigator Krantz came right out of his office when he heard who was there.

"I just heard the terrible news, and I want you to know I was on the island yesterday afternoon visiting my mother," Huxley said. "I left her house about four-thirty and caught the next launch."

"Anything else?" asked the investigator.

"Tessa and I were close a while back," Huxley said.

"So I understand. Did you see her on Sunday?"

"No."

"I'm sure you realize I'll have to check out your story."

"Of course. Not a problem. Harriet Soong. Unit three zero one."

"You've saved me some trouble, Mr. Soong. Thanks for coming in."

"You're welcome, Investigator. Let me know if you have other questions."

"Here's one. Ever run into a guy named Roy Desroy?"

"Don't think so," answered Huxley.

"Here's another. Who murdered Tessa Posnoff?"

Huxley shrugged. "What makes you so sure she was murdered?"

"What makes you so sure she wasn't?" Krantz asked.

On his way home Huxley omniplussed his mother. No answer. It was late—she was probably asleep. He left a message. "Omniplus me," he said. "ASAP."

TUESDAY, AUGUST 15, 2073

Melody tried to visualize her future children but instead saw Roy, his big hands and chest, his sandy hair, freckles, and especially his mouth, kissing his mouth, breath sweet as the air around pine trees. His looks had reassured her—how could someone so solid and strong with eyes so clear and intelligent not make a wonderful mate? They weren't the looks of someone who was insincere, someone who would hurt her. Before he dumped her, he was the man she wanted to father her children. Although, she reminded herself before she fell asleep, not any more.

From now on, she firmly told herself, you must be really careful and only fall in love with an upright man. But how can you tell what someone's really like? Granny would have said,

"You can't, little darling. Not till you live with him at least five years, by which time you've got kids, cats, dogs, a house to clean, and dinner to cook. I'd call that too late."

Or, *"You'll know he's the right one when he kisses you and you faint dead away."* Forget it; she'd never have said that. More like, *"Face it, sweet darling, life's a crapshoot. Always has been, always will be, and there's no way you'll win, however well you play. Get your children under your belt—that's the important thing and what nature wants."*

And that's what Melody wanted almost as much as she wanted to be a famous singer-songwriter, and for the latter to happen she was going to have to be nicer to

Huxley—a lot nicer. He was her only contact in the music world. From now on, she would pretend his remarks were cute and funny. She would flirt with him. Yes. As for Lionel—she must have been crazy to think he could advance her career, that he even knew anyone in the music business—his connections, if he ever had any, were too old or long dead.

Melody had been flattered that Lionel even noticed her and stunned he'd come to her defense. No one had ever done that before. It had felt good but it had also confused her. Made her think he loved her and she, him. What to do? She didn't want to be rude. Had she flirted with him? She supposed so. Flirting came to her as naturally as breathing, unless she consciously turned it off—as with Huxley.

It struck her that she fell for anyone who was really nice to her. That is—if he was also attractive.

She looked at her watch. She had to hurry if she was going to be on time for her appointment.

There hadn't been a murder for twenty-six years in Sywannah, and the police had to pretend they weren't excited when interviewed by Planetary Press International, which distributed its footage to all the papers and channels on the globe and beyond.

"The victim, Tessa Posnoff, was a sex specialist at Pine Haven, one of HEAVEN's facilities," Investigator Krantz told the press.

"Sex specialist?" asked a delighted reporter.

"Yes, I'm not certain what her duties were, but I'll find out and let you know. Here are the remaining facts as we've received them thus far. She was twenty-nine years old and lived in the Service area of Pine Haven. A dog belonging to Sarah Rally, a resident of Pine Haven, discovered the victim's body in Winding River near the airstrip. Zack Dakota, a pilot, was next on the scene, then Lionel Questar, former senator and one of our Living Treasures, who lives on the island.

"The victim died sometime between four and five o'clock on Sunday, the thirteenth of August. Her next of kin is a younger sister, Annemarie Posnoff, of St. Michelle. Owing to Ms. Posnoff's understandable shock and grief, she has requested another two days of privacy before answering your questions."

"Won't the trail go cold?"

"No, our recently appointed grief captain is with her and will find out any pertinent information as to the people in Tessa's life who her sister thinks might have had something to do with her death."

"You mean, murdered her."

"Well, yes, you could put it that way."

"What was the cause of death?"

"According to the coroner, she was struck on the back of the head several times with a sharp, hard object."

"How did she end up in the water?"

"That's part of the investigation. We don't know at this time."

"Where was she killed?"

"We don't know at this time."

"The Administration has given us one picture of Tessa taken when she applied for a job several years ago. Do you have access to more recent ones?"

"Sorry, we're looking and will field them to you when and if there's a discovery. I'm afraid that's all we have to say at this time."

"What about boyfriends? From the looks of her, she must have had a few."

"Be assured we're looking into it. That will be all. Thank you."

"Just one more question, Investigator. We understand she had many friends in Swyannah. Were you one of them?"

"Just about everyone knew Tessa, but I doubt many considered themselves her friends. Certainly I didn't."

"Enemies, then?"

The investigator shook his head and looked disgusted. "Enough," he said and waved the reporter off as he went into his office where Lionel and Zack sat, listening to every word.

"Sounds like someone wants *your* timeline, Investigator," Lionel said.

"Oh yeah? Well, he can have it. If I did the deed, you'd be looking at the most surprised cop in the South."

"Would you arrest yourself?" Zack asked.

"You're damn right. Now let's have those timelines."

He was a slow reader but their reports didn't require more than a glance.

Shit, he thought, *neither of them could have done it.* "You realize I can't be sure these are correct until I check with the hospital."

"Fine with us," Lionel said. "It's God's truth."

"We'll see. Now tell me how am I going to find that Roy fellow? I've thought all along he was probably the one who did it. He flew off the island at the right time."

"Tessa knew a lot of men," Zack said. "It would be a challenge to come up with all their names."

"Yeah, well isn't that too bad? It's a challenge you'll have to meet, Mr. Dakota. You too, Senator. I want you both here tomorrow morning at eight o'clock with every name you can think of."

"I have to work," Zack said.

"Oh yeah, what do you do?"

"I fly the Finals to the Stratadrome."

"Does that make sense to you, Senator?"

"Afraid not."

"Me either, but please don't explain, Mr. Dakota. I don't like the sound of it."

"Sorry," Zack said, "I can't change my job description."

"Of course you can't, Mr. Dakota. What do you say I write you an excuse?" Investigator Krantz said. "You'll have a day off. What could be better than spending it here with me?" He struck the side of his thigh as he noted a thought taking form in his brain. "You'll be my deputy. I may need a pilot."

Annemarie was in the fetal position, her head invisible under the covers, when Zack returned from Swyannah. She had cried hard and long in his arms the night before until exhaustion took over and she fell asleep. He had watched over and comforted her in his bed for a while— then collapsed on the living room couch. He'd had only a few hours of sleep before meeting Lionel at seven forty- five to take the skimplane across the bay for their appointment with Krantz.

Zack wondered what he was going to do with her when she woke up. He had to find another place for her to stay while she was on the island. He wasn't a goddamn saint, after all. She was so sweet and sad and smelled so good that he'd come close to screwing her last night. She probably wouldn't have objected. Thank God he had restrained himself. He would have screwed himself as well. He was supposed to love Melody. He did love Melody.

He looked up the Swyannah listings for the last names of men who must have known Tessa on his omniplus. It was meaningless to give them to Krantz. If any of them had been on the island, there would have been a record and Krantz would already know. Those robots didn't mess up. Krantz was desperate. *He needed a viable suspect,* Zack thought, *and the only one who made any sense was Tessa's ex-boyfriend.* He doubted Annemarie would know a thing about Roy, but he would ask. She would want to find out who killed Tessa even more than Krantz.

"Tomorrow may be too late to catch up with him, so let's go now," Annemarie said, after she had a piece of toast and two cups of tea. As it turned out, she knew all about Roy Desroy because Tessa had omniplussed her twice a day, minimum, and Tessa had believed her affair with him would develop into a long-term relationship, like marriage. In the time they were together, Roy had confided in Tessa and made promises. His family was from Darby, a small southern town, and he was tight with them, especially his mother and cousins. They'd know where he was. They didn't have to know Roy was a suspect in Tessa's death.

"Got to be back before four," Zack said. "I have to work."

"We'll be back in time if we leave now."

He was amazed Annemarie was so clear-headed. Had she cried herself out? What a relief. But she wasn't nearly as appealing to him now, back as straight as the omniplus in her hand, texting a list.

"Okay, we'll need an address," Zack said.

"I've got it." Annemarie waved her omniplus in the air. "Reach, directions, the whole bit."

"I'm impressed. You really know how to operate that thing. You must have an enhanced version," Zack said.

Upon admission, each resident of Pine Haven received a

number that would accompany them ten years later to the StrataDrome, HEAVEN's Final resting place. Surnames were not in general use. The official explanation was that it was simpler to remember a first or nickname. The actual reasoning was that identification with an ethnic group could predispose the employees and residents to favor or disfavor someone. And an ethnic surname was seldom synonymous with a person's genetic make-up anymore, so why bother with it? Someone with an Irish last name might be one-quarter Swedish, one-quarter Native American, one-quarter Jewish, one-eighth African-American, one-sixteenth Latino and one-sixteenth Irish. Thus, the name on Melody's new client folder was Harriet, not Harriet Soong.

Melody swallowed a meal pill whole after holding it in her mouth long enough to taste its orange flavor. As she walked to the Departure Pavilion, the meal pill expanded little by little, so by the time she arrived, her stomach felt full. There were days when she only had meal pills. They were convenient and supplied her with all necessary vitamins, minerals and fiber. Even before Roy dumped her, she'd been losing her desire and taste for food. Not a bad thing—eating took up too much time.

Inside the empty Departure Pavilion, she compared the handwriting of the mystery note with two of Zack's signatures and several of his memos. A through Z, there wasn't one similar letter. That meant the sender was either Lionel or Huxley, unless it was someone she hadn't thought of yet. She would see Huxley at rehearsal on Thursday and could ask him to sign something then—his picture perhaps. That would flatter him and not seem too odd.

Then there was Lionel. He must have signed his name to some paperwork at the hospital. Melody was sure one of her friends would let her look in the files. Right now, she had to get over to meet Harriet, her client-to-be. Once Sarah Departed, Harriet would take her place on the master schedule, but now that Sarah was in the hospital and might die before her appointed time, the Prolocutor said Melody and Harriet might as well get acquainted.

"A head start," she said.

Melody had seen Harriet briefly after her arrival when she was in the hands of the Greeters, before she was assigned a temporary Angelic. She remembered a slim, shapely, elderly woman with jade-green eyes in a lavender dress. It would be Melody's job to find out her history, interests, past illnesses or troubles and become prepared to medicate her if necessary for depression or inappropriate elation.

Also, she would make appointments for Harriet's periodic doctor check-ups. She would be Harriet's secretary, nurse and impersonal confidante. In ten years, if Melody still worked at Pine Haven, she would release Harriet from life on earth in a state of ecstasy, as guaranteed by the state.

At nine forty-five, Investigator Krantz was writing in his book after leaving Harriet's apartment. Melody smiled at him. "Good morning," she said.

"Good morning," Krantz replied and showed his ID. "We're investigating a death. I suppose you've heard we discovered a body here last night."

"No," Melody said. "Right here?"

"No, I mean in the river."

"Do you know whose body it is?" Melody asked.

"Yes. Tessa Posnoff."

"Oh my God!" Melody gasped. "Are you sure? I don't believe it."

"Why don't you believe it?"

"I don't know. It just seems impossible. Such things don't happen." Krantz's directness flustered Melody. Somehow, she felt she looked guilty.

"You obviously knew her," Krantz said.

"She works—worked here, I work here. We know—knew each other."

"Did you like her?" Krantz's eyes drilled into Melody's.

"Not really. She took my boyfriend away." *Not that it's any of your goddamn business*, she thought.

"I appreciate your honesty." He wrote in his book. "When was that?"

"A while back."

"What was your boyfriend's name?"

"Roy Desroy."

"Do you know where he is?"

"No."

"We need to talk more. When are you finished for the day?"

"About four-thirty, depending."

"Depending on what?"

"How long the Finals take."

"There's that word again. Dammit. What's a Final?"

"A corpse, Investigator. A resident who just died."

"I see." He wrote it in his book. "I'd like to see you in my office after work. And please bring a timeline for Sunday."

"A what?"

"Where you were during the day and evening."

"Why?"

"We think Tessa was murdered."

"By me?" She could feel her face redden.

"Who knows? Say, are you going in to see Mrs. Soong?"

"Mrs. Who?"

"Soong. Say," he said, pen ready, "I forgot to ask. What's your name?"

Melody didn't know who the woman was who opened the door. Later, she'd recognize the green eyes, but Harriet's transformation was extraordinary and total.

"You look great," was all Melody could think of to say when Harriet identified herself. "Just great."

"Thank you," Harriet said. "But I feel as if I've disappeared. It's strange."

"It must be," Melody said.

"Would you like an iced fizz?" Harriet asked, moving toward her tiny kitchen.

"Sounds good," Melody said.

"The investigator didn't want one. He just wanted to ask me questions about my son."

"Why?" Melody asked.

"He was here Sunday afternoon." Harriet said. "The police believe that poor woman was killed some time after four o'clock."

"Did your son know Tessa?"

"So the investigator said. He said they were close for a long time."

"Oh." Melody frowned.

"I never knew about it—but then he never tells me anything about his private life. To tell you the truth, I'm glad to know he had a girlfriend, though, of course, I'm sorry about what happened to her."

"It's horrible," Melody said.

"Did you know her?"

"Yes. She was an employee here." Melody hoped that was all she wanted to know about Tessa. It wasn't her place to criticize—and she probably would if Harriet wanted to know what Tessa was like.

Harriet handed Melody the fizz. "Well, I suppose you have questions for me, too."

Melody hesitated. "You're right. But they can wait if you'd rather."

"No, go ahead."

"I'd like to know about you. Anything you care to tell me. Your life story, if you feel like it," Melody said.

"You're the first person who ever wanted to hear it."

"Well, I do."

"Are you sure?" Harriet asked.

"Positive."

"Okay, well, may I get you anything? Are you comfortable?"

Melody nodded.

"Okay, here goes."

Harriet started her story, with Melody only half-listening. What should she do? If Harriet were related to Huxley, Melody had to tell her their connection before she said anything too personal.

"Excuse me, Harriet. I'm sorry to interrupt."

"That's all right, dear."

"Soong isn't a common name, you know. I know a Huxley Soong. Is he any relation?"

Harriet smiled. "Yes. My son. What a coincidence. How do you know him?"

"I'm the female singer with the CrossOvers."

"What's that?"

"Your son's group. Surely you know about it."

"Not the name but, yes—I know he has a band. He just told me."

"Well," Melody said. "I thought you should be aware that Huxley and I knew each other before you told me anything too personal." Melody hoped she didn't look embarrassed.

"Why?" Harriet asked.

"You might have been uncomfortable if you found out after the fact."

"How thoughtful." She smiled at Melody. Her teeth were a blinding white and perfectly even.

"Now, where was I?"

It didn't take long for Harriet to tell Melody her life story. It was mostly so ordinary, except for her husband's fame and untimely death. After his death, she'd immersed herself in her career. She'd had relationships but never wanted to marry again. She'd played word and number games on the LimitLessLink, read history, biography and cookbooks. Once upon a time she'd cut out recipes, most of which she never made because neither Huck nor Huxley cared about food; they ate to live.

After Huxley moved to Swyannah, she became known among her friends for mini-feasts of highly seasoned and grilled seafood, wild salmon, and roasted mixed vegetables, followed by her signature chocolate soufflé. Her friends would have been even more amazed if she'd told them she had a secret passion.

"Goodness, how exciting," Melody said. "What was it?"

"Tap dancing," Harriet said with a shy smile.

Melody was momentarily speechless. Then she said, "Well, as my granny would say, Lord love you."

Harriet was pleased. "I understand there's a Dance Center here."

"I'll walk you over. You can talk to the Head. She'll know how to fit you right in."

"If there aren't tap classes, maybe I could teach one."

Melody was momentarily speechless again. "You must be really good," she said finally.

"I've been doing it a long time." Harriet stood up, stretched down, touched the floor and did a time-step. "Of course, it's better with music and tap shoes," she said.

"Does Huxley know this?"

"He'd think I was crazy."

Melody nodded unconsciously. She'd think her mother, more than thirty years younger than Harriet, was crazy, too, if she took up tap. She caught herself. "It's just that Huxley probably thinks of you as…um…"

"An old lady. Why wouldn't he? That's what I am, even if I look a lot younger and more attractive than I did."

"I think you're amazing," Melody said. "You know, I love those old musicals. I used to watch them all the time."

"That's what got me started. Tap looked like so much fun."

Harriet shuffle-ball-changed twice, did a buck and wing, several flaps and a stomp.

Melody closed her file. "Wow," she said.

The omniplus awoke Huxley. It was his mother.

"Mom," he said. "I've got a favor to ask."

"If it has to do with the investigator who was here asking questions, it's too late."

"What do you mean?'

"When he asked which path you took to go to the launch, I told him the one to the left. I didn't know why he asked, but now I think I do."

"I didn't have anything to do with Tessa's death, Mom."

"I know, but he's going to be sure you saw her."

"Oh God."

"Why didn't you say something to me? I could have told him I didn't notice," said Harriet.

"I left a message for you to omniplus me."

"I just heard it. Sorry." There was a long pause. "It's just as well. The truth is best."

"But maybe I didn't go all the way to the dock. Maybe I turned back."

"If that's a lie, you'll just get into trouble," said Harriet.

"You don't think being a suspect in Tessa's murder isn't trouble?"

"Yes, but you didn't do it, and the truth will come out."

"Shit."

"What, dear?"

"I hope you're right. I'll talk to you later."

Huxley was thinking as fast as he could. Shit. Why didn't he tell the truth to begin with? He had a dozen reasons, but would Krantz be sympathetic? Not a chance. He was toast.

Lionel examined Sarah's pale, smooth face as she lay asleep in the hospital bed under a thin green blanket, arms out, partly bandaged. Covering what? He thought she'd just had pneumonia—nothing else. Had she fallen? He thought about how much he liked her, and since his brain surgery, how little he liked himself. The man he was getting to know by listening to his voice telling his life story wasn't an appealing person.

Except for Ginger, Louella and Billy, it was clear he'd never mourned anyone. He'd handled his feelings as if they were in a package on a shelf and too tightly wrapped to get inside, even if he wanted to.

It was upsetting to think Sarah would Depart in eleven days. It occurred to him, not for the first time, that if he married Sarah, she could live as long as possible and continue to enjoy the best of care.

The only problem was—he didn't want to get married.

Marriage had never worked out for him, and had brought terrible luck to his wives. He had promised himself, never again. Still, it was something to consider, though Sarah might not even like the idea.

"What's today?" Sarah asked, her eyes opening suddenly.

"Tuesday," Lionel told her.

"I want to get up."

"Easy now, you've been very sick."

"Thank goodness you're here," Sarah said.

Before Lionel, who felt warmth forming in his chest at her words, could answer, she continued. "I need your help."

"You've got it," said Lionel.

"I'm not ready to die."

"So you told me. I wouldn't be either."

"But everyone has to think I'm dead."

"Okay."

"I thought if I went for a swim and were eaten by a shark, they wouldn't look for my body."

"What shark?"

"I don't know. The other day, Tom warned me that there were sharks just waiting for a good meal."

"Who's Tom?"

"The lifeguard who used to work here. Never mind. Is it so farfetched to think there are sharks in the ocean?"

Lionel shook his head.

"The other possibility is if I drowned or seemed to, you could pick me up in your boat, take me to shore upstate and fly me to some little New England town."

"Okay. Then what?"

"Then, with your help, I'd cash in my security diamonds, one by one. That's it."

"Security diamonds? Okay. But it seems to me there are some gaps."

"Maybe so, but we can work them out, don't you think?"

"I don't know, Sarah. It's pretty wild."

"I suppose," Sarah said.

"I need to think it over." Lionel patted her arm.

"Of course you do." Sarah sat up, her aqua eyes tight on Lionel's face. "How long will it take?"

In the early afternoon, Ben had settled himself in the shadow of Lionel's house between a bed of daylilies and the tufted lawn of sea grass and sand. Although it was unlikely Krantz would ask him for a Sunday timeline, it was best to be prepared. He could, of course, be absolutely honest. On the other hand, being partly honest might work better since he didn't want to give Lionel away if, indeed, it had been Lionel at the dock. And he didn't want to say he saw Lionel after four o'clock or mention the recording. He could say he'd gone for a stroll around four-thirty and heard loud voices coming from the dock. He could say by the time he got there, he didn't see anyone. It wasn't as if Tessa's body would have been visible, unless he went out on the dock, and why would he have done that? He had to admit he wasn't just protecting his friends; he was protecting himself, his reputation. He had seniority and could do pretty much as he liked. He never pulled guard duty; he could miss meetings if he liked.

All that would be over. In fact, he might be over. What would stop the Administration, or Roy, from taking out all his parts, recycling them and throwing his outsides on the junk heap or even worse, changing his innards completely so he looked like, but was no longer, Ben?

He should have notified the Administration as soon as he discovered Tessa's body. None of the other robots would have been so derelict. If his sin of omission was ever discovered, the Administrators, Roy and his human friends would look at him and say, "Ben, how could you?" He didn't want that. He'd have to go for the partial truth.

It struck him that this was an example of his becoming more like a human and less like a robot. Humans told lies all the time to protect themselves, and didn't even notice they were lies, unless under oath. Even then they told lies, or so he'd heard. Humans had many more faults than virtues, and yet Ben found the two-legged creatures irresistible. He wanted to protect them, especially the ones he cared about. He supposed it was only natural he would pick up some of their ways.

Meanwhile, he comp-wrote another page of notes for his dissertation-in-progress, *Deconstructing the Human Experiment*; A Hermeneutical Underview.

1. Humans have feelings that get in the way of accomplishing much in their foreshortened day. At least eight hours are spent asleep; four hours, eating and drinking; three hours exercising, bathing, showering, getting dressed, undressed and looking in the mirror; which leaves nine hours to do things. For at least six of those hours, they are feeling angry, happy, repentant, sorrowful, excited, amazed, sexy, hurt, jealous, loving, bored, frustrated, disgusted, afraid, or ashamed. There was a time when I didn't understand any of these emotions and, no doubt, that's why they seemed so unnecessary. Now I understand happy, worried, ashamed, amused and repentant.

2. Imagine the time humans could utilize if they weren't so emotional.

3. Humans are capable of murder. Jealousy, greed fear, and anger are the most common reasons for such an action. If Tessa were murdered, it was for one of those reasons.

4. Humans can't imagine they will die, even though they know it's a given.

5. The people at Pine Haven know when they are going to die. Some of them would probably be hysterical as the day approaches, but powerful drugs calm them.

6. Most humans love to eat. They also love to talk about what they ate, or what they are going to eat.

7. Maybe I understand loving. Not sure.

8. If I learn to understand anger, would that mean I'd be capable of murder?

9. Humans are a lot of fun. Robots, myself excluded, are not.

10. If I could change into a human, would I? Food for thought, but I don't think so.

11. What if I could change into a real crocodile? No. Crocodiles are disgusting, ferocious and without any comprehension of the civilized world.

12. I suppose I could act as if I feel things. From what I've downloaded, you become what you pretend to be.

13. A human would say change is both interesting and desirable. Maybe.

14. Ben Franklin took one virtue at a time and worked on it until he was its master. I could try that with emotions.

When Melody passed him, Ben didn't notice. He was fixated on anger.

"What's the matter with Ben?" Melody asked Lionel. She had come by his house to give Babe a treat on her way to see Sarah in the hospital. Melody had a gift for her, a new blockbuster called *The Karamazov Plot*. She'd seen the book, *The Brothers Karamazov,* at Sarah's on Sunday and thought the title, at least, would amuse her.

"Nothing, so far as I know," Lionel said.

"He's grouchy as all get-out. I'd swear he growled at me."

"Ben doesn't growl."

"Okay, maybe not. Never mind, I'm off."

She picked up a pinecone and walked away, her long legs and short skirt improving Lionel's perfect view of the ocean, the copse of trees. Melody stopped. Her brief visit had been revealing. Lionel didn't act at all interested in her, which was a relief. There probably wasn't any reason to check out his handwriting. It wouldn't be his style to write a note and slip it under her door. Then again, it was possible. She dropped the pine cone and turned back.

"Say, Lionel," she said. "I forgot to ask. Did you have to write out a timeline for Krantz?"

"Don't remind me about that guy."

"I have to hand mine in right after work today."

Lionel's face said, "Why are you telling me this?"

"Just wondered if you'd mind if I used a piece of your paper and borrowed your pen?"

Lionel looked surprised and a little annoyed.

Melody flashed one of her knock-em-dead smiles. "I'm not going to have time to go home first."

Lionel reached into his desk. "Here you go." He sat back in his chair and frowned. "I sure don't understand the sudden popularity of my stationery."

"What do you mean?"

"This is the same paper and pen Zack used yesterday."

Same ink, same paper. Oh my God, Zack. It was Zack.

"You're looking a bit—I don't know—upset?" Lionel said. "Sit down, Melody, for Christ's sake."

"Poor Tessa," Melody said.

"Oh, that's what's bothering you." Lionel patted her shoulder. "Yes, it's awful. Try not to think about it."

Melody wrote out her timeline, a bit shakily, and returned his pen. "I'm all set. Thanks a lot," she said. She waved goodbye.

Once again, Lionel watched her long, graceful legs, as she walked into the copse of pine trees that hid the path to the hospital.

"Don't be an idiot," he murmured to himself.

Ben rounded the house. It was time to play with Babe and shoot the breeze with Lionel.

"Squalls expected after six this evening," Ben said. "Choppy seas all day."

It didn't take long for Lionel to complete his time-line. He remembered Sunday afternoon perfectly. But, he asked himself, was it necessary to put his trip home in his timeline? No one had seen him, including whoever it was he saw on his way back. Besides, he didn't kill Tessa, so what was the point of telling Krantz he had played hooky from the hospital sometime between four and four forty-five on Sunday afternoon? It would just muddy the waters and put him under suspicion, instead of narrowing the field. It would be foolish. Besides, he was no stranger to deception, having served in the House and Senate, run for president and cheated on his wife. You could say this would merely exercise an atrophying talent.

He wrote: Lionel Questar—Time Line: All day Sunday, August 13, 2073 — Hospital. Room 226.

On Monday morning, Harry of Maintenance had picked up the blanket, collapsible bag, nuts and chips and the empty intoxofloat bottle and glass left by Roy in the grass near the fishing dock. There was nearly always debris there, especially after a weekend. Early the next day, he received an omniplus from Investigator Krantz.

"Because of Ms. Posnoff's death, we're roping off the river," Krantz said. "Don't remove anything in, around or near it."

"Okay," said Harry, "but you're a little late. My men and I clean up first thing every morning, Monday through Friday."

"We think Tessa may have been murdered somewhere upstream and floated down."

"She definitely wasn't the type to stay put," said Harry.

"Very funny," Krantz said.

"This guy's a real jerk," he said, his hand over the omniplus, to his assistant.

"Did you fill out a timeline for me, sir?"

"You've got it. Harry Plato."

Krantz thumbed through a stack of papers. "Yeah, okay, it's here."

"Know-it-all little prick," Krantz said, after covering the omniplus again.

"Do you remember seeing anything unusual in the trash, Mr. Plato?"

"Not offhand, but I'll think about it and let you know."

Investigator Krantz nearly threw his omniplus across the room. The Plato guy made him mad. He was going to search the whole goddamn area himself. He needed to find out where it happened. He had Zack to thank for suggesting Tessa might have met her fate further upstream. In the excitement, it hadn't occurred to Krantz, God help him—it wasn't something he wanted his superiors to know.

It was late morning when Krantz walked up the river on the Pine Haven side. Exhibit bags, carried by his assistant were already full of junk that had been lying around for more than a day and had been missed by Harry and his Maintenance wonders. There were several bottles, always promising for imprinting, and some underclothing, a magazine and miscellaneous objects. At least he wasn't the only one who didn't do his job perfectly. He'd hardly slept the night before and was up, shaved, dressed, and ready for breakfast at six o'clock. This was his watershed moment. If he handled the case correctly, he'd be known all over the state and stand a good chance of a promotion.

As he went along, Krantz took stock of the other bank and the bottom of the river between. He scooped out anything floating with his net. He'd go down the other side later. The fishing dock was about halfway to the end of the river proper. After that, it split into creeks and canals and went out to sea. The boards protested as Krantz charged out on the dock and peered into the water. The water was clear.

"What's that?" he asked his assistant—pointing to a just visible blue object under the water.

"Don't know. I'll get it, sir," the assistant said, standing a few feet behind him near the shack where he propped the bags. He was wearing boots, but this looked to be deep. He removed his boots and socks, rolled up his pants as high as he could and slipped off the shallow end of the dock. The water was cold.

The object had dug deep into the heavy sand. His assistant plunged his hand into the water pulled it out carefully. "It's a book," he said. "Completely ruined."

"My first piece of good news," Krantz said.

"Why?" his assistant asked

"Because someone bought or borrowed it," Krantz said. "Which means I'll be able to find out who that was."

The assistant was soaking wet. He put the book in an evidence bag. "Hey," he said. "There's a bubble-glass by the door. Looks like it's half full of something."

"I'll take it in myself," Krantz yelled, steaming his way back to the boathouse. "There's bound to be physical evidence. Signal emergency to pick us up right away. This may be it."

He put on a fresh pair of plastic gloves, opened a small padded box from his backpack and carefully placed the glass upright inside. He smelled it. "Intoxofloat." He chuckled. "Now we're cooking. Signal a team to rope off this entire area." He swung his arm in a large arc.

After the fingerprint examination, Krantz omniplussed to check on Tessa's blood alcohol level. Later, he'd omniplus the library. The pages were ruined, indecipherable, but the title on the cover was plain—*The Brothers Karamazov*. Not something Krantz had heard of. If it was a library book, the librarian would tell him who borrowed it. No problem.

Except it was. The librarian was polite but firm. "I'll have to get permission from the borrower," she said in her tight voice.

Perhaps it gives her pleasure to say no to the police, he thought.

"We have a body here, and we need to find out why it isn't alive and walking around," Krantz said. "The book may be an important clue."

He interrupted her rote response about rules. "I'll omniplus the Prolocutor," he said.

The Prolocutor was back to him in minutes. "Sorry, but you'll need a subpoena."

"Okay, consider it done. The original will be in your hands in twenty minutes."

"All right then — but be sure you don't tell anyone gave you the information before it arrived."

"I won't."

"Good. Let's see. The book was checked out three days ago by Sarah Rally. Mrs. Rally is presently recuperating in the hospital."

"You're a sweetheart. Thank you very much."

The facts were mounting. There was a match on the glass with Tessa's fingerprints and DNA; her blood alcohol level had been .12. The drink was an intoxofloat made in Canada. Tessa had been very drunk, that was clear, but who'd been drunk with her? He omniplussed Harry Plato.

"We're looking for an intoxofloat bottle and a bubble-glass. You probably picked them up near the fishing dock yesterday morning."

"You're right, I did," Harry said. "I remember."

"You didn't find them unusual?"

"Heck, no. That's our local lovers' lane."

"I see." Krantz scratched his cheek. "Thanks. We'll find them," he said.

"Wait a damn minute," said Harry. "We've started loading the truck."

"Well stop."

"Jesus," Harry said and hung up.

Krantz didn't mind making another enemy. He omniplussed Harry back, Don't touch anything. My people are in charge of all your trash."

"Jesus," Harry said again.

Krantz didn't look forward to his interview with Sarah Rally. He knew she was almost ninety-five, had narrowly escaped pneumonia and had sustained nasty wounds on her shoulder, arms and legs that she refused to discuss. But he knew very little about the island and what went on there. Before Tessa's death, there was no reason to investigate. He promised the nurse he wouldn't say anything to upset Sarah, but then he did.

"Mrs. Rally, this won't take long. It's about a book." He watched her reaction.

Sarah sat up in her bed, nodded and said, "Go on."

"You borrowed *The Brothers Karamazov* from the library on Saturday. Is that correct?"

"I'm not sure of the day, but yes, I borrowed it."

"Do you know where it is?'"

She was unflappable. "In my bedroom, I think."

"Do you have any idea how it came to be in the river by the fishing dock?"

"The river? Oh my, let's see if I can remember. My short-term memory isn't so hot."

That expression reminded Krantz of his grandmother. "No hurry," he said.

"I like to read on the dock," she said.

"Yes, I understand." He always said that whether he did or not.

"So I must've taken it there."

"When?"

"Let's see. Sunday in the afternoon, after my nap."

"You're doing great, Mrs. Rally."

"Thanks."

"Did you forget to bring the book home with you?"

"I must have." She smiled and shrugged. "I don't know how it got in the water. The librarian is going to be furious."

"Don't worry about that."

"I can't imagine you've come all this way to ask me about a book, Investigator."

"The funny thing is I did, because it may have something to do with another question."

"What's that?" asked Sarah.

"Was Tessa Posnoff at the dock when you were there?"

"Tessa? Why? Did she say I was?"

"No, she didn't say anything."

"Then why?"

"You haven't heard?"

"Heard what?"

"Tessa's dead."

"Dead," Sarah said. "Tessa's dead?" She fell back onto her pillow.

Krantz nodded. "I thought surely you knew."

"When did it happen?"

"Sunday afternoon."

"My God." She found a tissue and wiped her eyes. "I'm sorry, Investigator, but this is quite a shock. I have to ask you to leave."

"Just one question, Mrs. Rally. Did you see Tessa on Sunday?"

Sarah closed her eyes. "I'll be glad to answer, but not now."

"Don't you want to know how she died?"

"If I have to."

"She was hit on the back of the head several times. We believe she died instantly. We also believe it was murder."

"And you think I killed her?" she asked.

"We don't know who did, but at this point, everyone's a suspect."

"You might as well pin it on me. After all, I'm scheduled to Depart in less than two weeks."

"Depart?" Krantz asked.

"Die. That's the deal."

Melody examined the stationary during the ride by skimboat to Swyannah. There was no question the paper and ink were the same. Exactly. It didn't look like Zack's handwriting on the note, but it was clear—Zack loved her. It was odd he didn't show up at the Pavilion this afternoon, but then there weren't any Finals to fly. Still, he usually came just to be sure, or maybe, she now realized, to see her. Funny he didn't check in to see if she were wearing gold and black.

Hey Granny, are you listening? A really nice person says he loves me, but I need to know if it's for real, if he's the right one and how I feel about him. I'm not sure. Please help. Send me a sign or something. I've been looking for someone who truly cares for me, but don't I need to care back? Does it matter he feels more like a friend than a lover? You'd probably say there's nothing wrong with that. Well, maybe I can fall in love with him later. It's funny not to feel he's a challenge—He's already been won over without my even flirting with him, or at least not intentionally. It's strange and kind of nice, but I'm waiting for a sign.

Melody was about to enter the precinct, her Sunday timeline in hand to give to Krantz. It was a pretty simple one, mostly dog-sitting with Babe, or talking with Sarah, or visiting Lionel in the hospital. Melody never dreamed she'd be a suspect in a murder case. It was sort of exciting, really.

"Who else is a suspect, Investigator?" Melody asked.

"Everyone." He sat behind his desk, eating a bagel and talking with his mouth full.

"That's a lot of people." She sat down uninvited.

He took another bite. "I mean, everyone who knew Tessa and could have seen her on Sunday."

"Okay, and that includes?"

"Your ex-boyfriend, Roy Desroy. Oh, by the way, it would be a big help," he sipped some water, "if you'd tell me where Roy might be." He coughed heavily. Sipped more water. "Then there's Huxley Soong, Zack Dakota, Lionel Questar, though the last two have perfect alibis, and Sarah Rally."

"You're kidding about Sarah, right?"

"Not at all. She saw Tessa at the fishing dock on Sunday afternoon."

"How do you know?"

"She told me. First she sent me packing and then omniplussed me with her story. So far, she's the only person who's admitted seeing Tessa on Sunday."

"Okay, but so what? Sarah wouldn't kill anyone."

"I'm just following procedure and that means I don't make any assumptions. In my book, Sarah could have done it. By the way, does she drink?"

Melody looked into Krantz's eyes with disbelief. "No, and she's nearly ninety-five years old. Not exactly the profile for a murderer."

"I was told her age but to me she doesn't look fifty."

"If she were fifty, she wouldn't be Departing in less than two weeks."

"You mean dying? I don't understand what's going on over there. Mass suicide? It sure sounds weird."

"Haven't any of your relatives gone to HEAVEN?" Melody asked.

"I hope so."

"No, I mean the place on earth for people from eighty-five to ninety-five. It's a national program. There are ads everywhere. I thought everyone knew about it."

"Okay. You're right. It rings a bell but for some reason I never paid attention. Maybe because no one in my family has ever lived past seventy."

"Sorry to hear that. Well here's my timeline," Melody said. "Let me know if you have any questions."

"I sure will, Ms. Graves."

"Actually, I do have a question, Inspector," Melody said.

"Shoot."

"I'm wondering if our advertising has been at all successful. Did you see the piece about our band, The CrossOvers"

"It sort of rings a bell."

"Well, I'm hoping maybe you and your wife will come see us sometime. I'm the singer and Huxley's the lead guitarist. Did you know that?"

Krantz shook his head.

"There are three shows every Friday and Saturday night starting at eight. We're pretty popular."

"Wait a minute. Weren't you the reason the senator punched that guy out the other night at the café?"

Melody tried not to smile but she couldn't help it. "Yes I was, Investigator. It was the first time it ever happened. To me, I mean."

"Then you must be Zack Dakota's fiancée. If it weren't for Zack explaining why the senator hit that guy, he would be in jail or out on bond. I knew you must be something special. Zack promised to bring you by so I could meet you. He's sure crazy about you."

"He is?"

Krantz smiled. "As if you didn't know. He's a good man. You're both lucky."

"What a lovely thing to say, Investigator," Melody said. She felt like giving him a kiss. "Sure hope I see you some Friday or Saturday. And your wife, too. Don't forget now."

Melody walked outside and looked up at the lavender sky. "That was fast, Granny," she said.

Okay, I got the sign—so now what? she thought. I guess I have to wear that black and gold scarf and see what happens. Seems pretty silly to me. So maybe I won't. Maybe when I see him, I'll just say, hey, Zack, thanks for the note or I got your poem or... Oh, the hell with it. I'll wear the damn scarf."

Roy's mother's front yard was a hodge-podge of statuary, mostly gnomes and animals, interspersed with chickweed and purslane. The house was one-story, painted off-white stucco, paint peeling. On the front porch in a swinging davenport suspended from huge screws on the ceiling sat an enormous, moon-faced woman.

"Well, hello there," she called. "What can I do for you?"

"We're looking for Roy Desroy," Zack said.

"That's my son, but he's not here." She fanned herself with a lurid-looking magazine.

"Could you give him a message?"

"Sure thing. What?"

"We've got some bad news about his girlfriend, Tessa Posnoff."

The woman's tiny eyes opened a little wider.

Annemarie blew her nose into a tissue. She was okay until Tessa's name was mentioned. Tears began to fill her eyes.

"She's dead," Zack said.

"Well, that is bad news. He never even told me about her." She shifted herself, accompanied by squeaking chains all around.

Annemarie caught her tears in another tissue. "Any idea where he might be?" she asked.

"If you don't mind setting a spell, he should be back within the hour." She gestured left, her massive arm swinging curtains of flesh, to something hidden by the porch wall.

"Sounds good. Thank you." There were three plastic chairs where she'd pointed. Zack and Annemarie picked their way between flower-pots full of weeds and dead geraniums, up the concrete steps.

"How do you do, ma'am?" Zack said. He bent his head respectfully. The woman didn't offer her hand.

"Hi," Annemarie said. "I'm Tessa's sister."

"Sure sorry to hear the news," said the woman. "Please, set yourself down. I'd offer you some iced tea, but there's none made and once I set down for the afternoon, that's it till my nieces come to fix my supper and such."

"We're fine," Zack said. The chairs were dirty but substantial. They sat.

"How'd you find us? The woman asked. "Desroy was Roy's father's name, but my last husband was Burch." She fanned herself. "He died a while back," she explained as if asked.

Zack turned toward Annemarie. She said, "Roy told Tessa all about his family, and Tessa told me. She was looking forward to meeting you all someday."

Mrs. Burch snorted. "I'll bet," she said. "Well, one thing you can say for us, we don't put on airs. What you see is what you get, and that ain't much."

That tickled Mrs. Burch enough to threaten the imminent collapse of the swing. "Hee, hee."

"You okay?" asked Annemarie.

"Hee, hee." Mrs. Burch fanned her purple-red face. "Laughing never hurt nobody. Say there, honey, was your sister as pretty as you?"

"People say we look a lot alike." Annemarie pushed her dark red hair back and circled it with a small scarf from her pocket. It was hot.

"What a shame," Mrs. Burch said.

Annemarie looked surprised.

"What I mean is, it's a shame such a pretty girl has passed. Roy's going to hate it."

"I expect he will," said Zack.

"He should be here any time now," said Mrs. Burch. "Any time."

Lionel studied his notes:

Choose day when weather is iffy.
Take hydroboat for a spin every day at different times.
Find a place to dock upstate near an airstrip.
Fly plane to airstrip and back.
Take boat to dock and back.
Problem: On day of escape, will need someone (Zack?) to pick me up by plane or boat after I park the plane.
Open a safety deposit box for Sarah's diamonds. Give sign-in privilege and second key to someone (Zack?).
Take out money to give Sarah to start her venture. Keep locked in plane.
Ask Sarah if she will trust another person (Zack?) to help us. Need to do first.
Order disguises for Sarah from Monty's. Have sent same-day express.
Ask Melody for calming pills.
Load up on towels for boat and plane.
Check out towns in New England. Find a small house to rent near the shore.
Find a bank in the town. Open a joint account with Sarah as co-signer. Her security ID must not be primary.

Lionel was excited, or nervous, or both. This was crazy. He must be out of his mind to think of helping Sarah. No matter how careful he was, a screw-up was possible—something he would forget to do. If Sarah agreed to let Zack help them, then he could bounce ideas off him. It would, or might, be a help. No matter what, this was going to be expensive. He'd pay Zack double-time plus a bonus and he'd give Sarah money to get started in her new life.

It wasn't going to be easy to find a trustworthy person to buy her diamonds. Damn. He'd never done anything like this before. He felt like a thief, just thinking about it. Forget the diamonds. He had more than enough money to take care of Sarah.

Uh oh, he thought. *What if I die?* It was getting complicated. He couldn't will any money to Sarah; she wouldn't officially exist and then again, she would exist once her cover was blown because of the joint account. Okay, she'd need another security ID. How to do that? Christ! How do criminals manage? It wasn't an easy job. He felt a sudden admiration for embezzlers, con artists, and masters of deception.

There was only one solution. He and Sarah had to get married. "I don't want to," he said to Babe, "but it's the only sensible solution." Babe jumped on his lap. "I mean," he continued, "the other plan is just insane. It won't work. It makes me tired just to think about it and, guess what? I want to help her escape even less than I want to get married."

He hugged Babe and put her on the floor. "Good," he said. "It's decided."

The idea of losing his privacy wasn't pleasing and if he were to think about it much longer, he'd change his mind. He would go straightaway to the hospital and propose to Sarah.

"Now," he told Babe. "Right now."

When Lionel got to the hospital, Sarah was asleep.

"Marry me," he said anyway.

By evening, Lionel was relieved Sarah hadn't heard his proposal. He'd changed his mind and decided saving Sarah might actually be fun. He could always marry her if it didn't work out. He'd simplify the process; forget about ID numbers and bank accounts. He'd get Sarah out of the water somehow and go on from there. He sat in the chair by her bed. She was sitting up, excited, expectant.

"It's way too complicated, Sarah," he said.

The toned and rejuvenated muscles in Sarah's face sagged. She clasped her hands. "I understand," she said.

"But we'll do it anyway. Give it our best shot. What the hell."

"Oh, Lionel. Are you sure? You're not fooling?"

He wagged his finger at her. "Have faith, old girl," he said. "Now that I'm used to the idea it sounds like fun. We'll have a blast."

"What do you mean?"

"The challenge of meeting the challenge. We'll have to wing it from second to second and minute to minute and never know for sure if the Administration is on our tail or not."

He stood and positioned himself in front of the floor to ceiling mirror by her privacy closet and smiled at what he saw, his flushed face, fierce eyes, the muscular set of his jaw and shoulders.

"If nothing else it should keep the blood coursing through our limbs even more than HEAVEN's mini-mano massage before breakfast," he said.

Lionel kissed Sarah on the forehead before leaving. "We don't have a lot of time to get all our ducks in a row," he said.

Sarah said, "I know but could we possibly do it before my Celebration? I don't want to go through all that."

"Oh Sarah, I'll try—but it might be easier if you escape while it's going on."

"Why?"

"People will be distracted by all the activity."

"I see," Sarah said. "Good thinking."

"I'll be in touch."

Wilbur, repaired and smelling of fresh paint, preceded Roy down the sidewalk by the length of a song-chorus. The tiny robot had spent his first year listening to and downloading upbeat tunes to amuse others, especially Roy. He was small enough to accompany Roy almost anywhere, though not as small as the snoop-op, Roy's favorite robotic design to date.

There were dozens of pocket-size, no-color snoop-ops, most of them hidden at various locations on the island, Swyannah and Darby, a few awaiting placement. Roy didn't actually hide them; they were designed to hide themselves or blend in with the background, like miniature chameleons. They took pictures, created videos and recorded sounds within a twenty-foot radius. Roy accessed their information, protected by a complex choral password changed from time to time by him or Ben from an ordinary omniplus.

Roy's dream was to market the snoop-ops first to local and later federal law enforcement. For several months, Roy had gathered information to prove their usefulness. There were too many roboticians in the country and it was time for him to figure out a way to get ahead. Before he did anything else, Roy wanted to build his mother a house that would accommodate her ever-expanding person. He'd need to hire a caregiver and a caretaker. Expensive. He needed to hit it big.

Two days ago, he had brought the intoxofloat as requested by Tessa, and she had brought the bubble-glasses to the dock where they'd first made love, when the excess of their passion had obscured the sound of the streaming water in the background. This time he heard it.

Tessa, he realized when he allowed himself to think about Sunday afternoon, had expected a proposal and although he'd expected her to make a fuss, he hadn't expected the baby thing. Of course later he hadn't expected her to destroy Wilbur. Nor had he planned to bash her head in on the rocks. No way. It wasn't his nature to do such a thing. It was her laughing about Wilbur that had made him wild with rage to the point he didn't know what he was doing. He concluded that what had happened was completely unintentional and not really his fault.

Roy's whistled. It was his signal.

"Here he comes," Mrs. Burch said. "I knew he wouldn't be long."

Zack stood up, brushed the dirt from the seat of his pants and walked to the steps.

"Hey, Roy, honey, we got company."

"That's nice," Roy said.

"It would be, except they've come with bad news."

Zack met Roy at the bottom of the porch stoop. He put his hand out. "Hey, we've met before," Zack said. "You're the robot guy."

"That's me," Roy said. "And you're the fly boy. What's the bad news?"

Zack put his hand over his mouth as if to stop the words, "Your friend is dead." He paused. "Tessa."

"Jesus Christ. How can that be? She was fine on Sunday." He sat down on the stoop and looked as if he was going to cry. "Was it an accident? Must've been."

"We don't know for sure," Zack said. "But the investigator wants to talk to everyone who saw her Sunday afternoon."

"Okay. No problem." Roy put his big sandy-haired head in his big golden-skinned hands. He looked up. "Are you sure she's gone?"

Annemarie came out from the side of the porch. She was crying. "You loved her, didn't you, Roy?"

Roy jumped. Annemarie was a dead ringer for Tessa. The light amber skin, the gold-green eyes and dark red hair.

Annemarie saw his alarm. "I'm her sister," she said, and patted his shoulder.

"Annemarie," Roy said. "Tessa's baby sister. Oh, honey, I'm so sorry."

"Thanks. Me, too."

"You sure look like her."

"Ain't she the pretty one?" Mrs. Burch said. "I guess Tessa was too. It's a terrible shame."

"She was quite a woman," Roy said. "Quite a woman."

"She told me you were bringing her to Darby with you," Annemarie said.

"We had an argument," Roy said, "and parted company. While we were celebrating our anniversary, she got mad at me."

"I'll leave it to the investigator to ask you why," Zack said.

"I'm an open book," Roy said. "Tessa wanted to get married and I said we would, but not yet."

Annemarie nodded. "Tessa was counting on you," she said.

"Do you want to tell me how she died?" Roy asked.

"She was found floating face up in the river with the back of her head bludgeoned in," Zack said.

"I bet some people think I killed her."

"Did you?" Annemarie asked.

"Hell, no," Roy said, his chin jutting out. "Why would I do a thing like that?"

"Maybe you were angry," Zack said.

"Tessa's the one who was angry. Not me."

Mrs. Burch was nearly choking with indignation. The sagging mountain of her breasts heaved as she caught her breath. "My son," she sputtered. "My son would never…"

"Okay, Mom. You don't need to defend me or worry about this. People tend to jump to conclusions. I'll fly back, meet with the authorities and clear it all up."

"Great," Zack said.

"We'll be glad for your company," Annemarie said.

Roy appraised them both to let them know he wasn't fooled. "That's what you came for, isn't it?"

Annemarie and Zack were silent.

"You don't need to give me a ride, my friends." He pointed to the side of the house where his little custom-designed robot-ready heliozoomer sat. "I have my own transportation."

Ben was walking by the pavilion, Babe at rest on his back, when Melody emerged, a crease between her eyebrows. "Hey," he said.

They walked together toward the hospital. "Lionel's visiting Sarah," Ben said.

"Zack never showed up. That was a first. Where could he be?" Melody sighed and rearranged her black and gold scarf for the twentieth time.

"I saw him off late this morning," Ben said. "He was in a big hurry."

"Did he say anything?"

"Said he'd be back before four."

"Was that all?"

Ben paused. "Almost," he said finally.

"Well, it's after four now."

"He found Roy in Darby," Ben said. "I got a message from him."

Melody readjusted her scarf. "I feel like a damn fool wearing this thing. And it's too hot" She pulled on the scarf. "Did he take anyone with him?" Melody asked.

"Annemarie," he said.

"Who?"

"Tessa's sister."

Melody took off the scarf. "Men!" she said. "Well, never mind. Give me Babe. It's time for her dinner." Babe jumped into her arms. Melody pressed the little dog to her and threw the scarf into the trash outlet.

When Zack returned with Annemarie to the Pine Haven airstrip, Ben was there to greet him.

"Melody's looking for you," Ben said. "She was upset you didn't come to work and acted funny when I said you'd taken Annemarie with you on your trip."

"What do you mean, funny?" Zack asked. Ben was obtuse when it came to attraction between the sexes.

"She tore off the scarf she was wearing. Just as well—it was an ugly black and gold thing, and she threw it on the garbage inlet near the hospital. I thought that was peculiar."

"No kidding? Why, that's just wonderful news."

Ben wondered how he could make enough sense of it all so he could put it in his dissertation. He was beginning to realize that no amount of study would make him understand humans, although since the point was to observe them, perhaps it didn't matter. He could always change his title. He was a scientist using the scientific method.

Zack left a message for Melody to get in touch. "I found your scarf," he said.

The scarf was lying right on top of the submerged container yet to be sucked into the underground trash-pulverizer. There were gold metallic swirls looping through sheer black mock-chiffon.

Investigator Krantz released his belt. The good news was puffing him up, as if he'd already had his pre-lunch ice cream sundae. First Huxley arrived, sweating profusely and said he needed to adjust his timeline. Suave, dapper Huxley, damp and mopping his face with a pocket linen in the cool of Krantz's office. The investigator grinned.

"So you saw Tessa?"

"Right."

"Why didn't you say so before?"

"I didn't kill her so I didn't see the point of having my face all over the wall-to-wall. You watch—it's going to hurt business."

"Maybe it'll help. People love to hobnob with suspects."

"Is that what I am?"

"Of course—same as before when I didn't believe you."

Krantz enjoyed the dumfounded expression on Huxley's face.

"Now tell me what happened. Take your time."

In the late afternoon, Zack came in with Roy and Annemarie. He introduced them to Krantz as if they were guests at a party.

"Nice to meet you both," the investigator said. "Please sit down. I have a few questions."

Roy described his afternoon on Sunday. Not only was he with Tessa, he was also eager to tell about it, word for word.

"So you claim she was alive when you left her?"

"I'll say. Alive, mad as hell and more than a little tipsy—we'd been drinking intoxofloat."

So, thought Krantz later, *according to his timeline, Roy was with Tessa before Huxley arrived. Then Sarah arrived — though given her age, she was an unlikely suspect, so maybe Roy or Huxley returned later after Sarah left. Two things were certain—something violent occurred and Tessa was dead.*

After telling Krantz most of what he could remember not including his return to the dock, Roy went home and tuned in to the snoop-ops with his omniplus. He scanned them by date and time beginning Sunday, the thirteenth, at three o'clock. Every sound and action would be there, including the murder, if he could bear to watch it. He grabbed a beer and sat in his brown leather reclining chair. He had some listening, watching and editing to do.

Zack and Annemarie agreed it would be best if she didn't stay in Zack's apartment another night. He omniplussed the Prolocutor who, eager to resolve the whole horrible mess, was delighted to assign her a room. Pine Haven's reputation was at stake—the murder might even threaten the institution of HEAVEN itself. Obviously, Annemarie couldn't stay in Tessa's apartment; it was sealed off.

"Come on, Zack. Let's go get my things," Annemarie said. They walked to his apartment and went in.

Fifteen minutes later, Annemarie came out with her bag. She reached up to give Zack a kiss on his cheek. "I can find my way," she said. "Thanks for everything."

By then, Melody was on her way home. She'd seen them go in together. That was enough for her.

Okay Granny. Zack's changed his mind, or maybe he's just fickle, like all the guys I've ever known. So I guess

Zack isn't the guy for me. Maybe Huxley's the one. Oh Lord, listen to me! If it isn't Lionel, then it's Zack, and if it isn't Zack, then it's Huxley. That's what you'd say. Then you'd say it'll all work out for the best. Just be patient, you'd say. But it's not the way it used to be, Granny. It doesn't always work out.

There aren't a lot of guys who are willing to commit to a woman and the children they have together. Maybe I'm not special like you always said I was. It doesn't feel like I am. I feel like shit. I feel like having nothing to do with men ever again. I feel like becoming a nun. There are still such women who leave the world, pray, meditate and do good works. Please stop laughing. I'm serious.

Huxley decided he would have to start over, leave his beloved, chic apartment and move. He could take care of other people's property anywhere, find guitar students anywhere, though it would take a while to set up a band anywhere and find a singer as good as Melody. It would be more of an effort to see his mother, but once he got settled, he could move her to another, closer HEAVEN facility. In any case, she wasn't his primary concern. He needed to search for a community as much to his liking as Swyannah had been. But what if he were to be accused of Tessa's death? How could he prove he didn't do it? What if he were convicted, imprisoned? It was both inconceivable and terrifying.

He mixed himself a gin fizz, stretched out on his black-cushioned wicker chaise and began a list. It always made him feel better to make a list, even if he didn't follow it. The omniplus whistled. He didn't feel like talking to anyone. He heard his mother's voice. "I'm anxious to hear from you, dear," she said. "Bye."

Such a message would have annoyed him at one time—yesterday, for example—but today he was happy to hear her caring voice. Perhaps she'd always loved him in her way. As he mused about their life together in San Della, he saw what his defense would be. If he'd been really worried about his mother telling the investigator which path he took on Sunday, he would have made sure he reached her first thing Tuesday morning and told her what to say.

Whether that would be considered a defense against arrest or not, he'd still have to move away. His privacy, which he valued above all else, was about to be destroyed. Still, he was young enough to build a new life, although the aftermath of Tessa's death had tired him out, and for the first time, he considered his own mortality. He saw himself lying on a pallet, yellowish and rigid, with no one to mourn him. *But that would be years from now*, he told himself.

Too bad his aunt had passed on. She might have been able to read his future so he could plan ahead. He'd never done that. Every day was simple and much the same: he worked, taught, played the guitar and, whenever possible, screwed women. If he'd read about such a life, he'd have thought it was sad.

The southwest had always appealed to him. He'd been to El Toredo several years back. It attracted artists and writers, wannabe artists and writers, and people who invited both groups to their parties. It might be a pleasant place to set up shop.

Later, before falling asleep, Melody tried to remember exactly how it was she and Zack became engaged that night when, except for a working relationship, they hardly knew each other. She needed to know what story to tell their future children—if there were any. The setting played a part: a small, candlelit table by a window in an expensive seafood restaurant, cantilevered over the bay. So did an elegant dinner she couldn't finish or remember. But what played the biggest part was the bottle of verivinoggio they shared and polished off.

Halfway through the bottle, Zack's tongue loosened." I love you, Melody," he said. "I loved you the first time I saw you in Departure Pavillion, I love you now and I will always love you." He reached across the table for her hand. She let him hold it.

It would be rude not to, she thought.

"I dream of us living as man and wife, with three children, several dogs, a few cats, and a goat or two…"

"A goat or two?" Melody said. "Really?"

"Yes. But don't worry. I'll milk them and make the cheese."

"Where do you see us living?" Melody asked.

"The mountains," he said. Melody was silent.

"But that's just part of my plan. I've thought it through. Any fool would know a person as talented as you wouldn't be happy with just family and nature. You'd want to be where there are bright lights and audiences. Right?"

Melody nodded.

"Not a problem. I'll fly you wherever you want to go."

Melody was surprised. "Wait a minute. What about the children and animals?"

"We'll have helpers who can take over."

"Who will they be?"

Zack squeezed her hand. "Good people," he said and repeated, "Good people."

Like Zack, thought Melody. *Her parents would say Zack was 'good people.'*

Melody closed her eyes and saw herself joining Zack on his mountain. *I see it. It might be perfect—if he truly loves me. Maybe he does. Granny must believe he does or she wouldn't have sent that sign and I wouldn't be here.*

"I shouldn't have had that last glass," Melody said. She stood and took hold of the back of her chair. "I may need your arm."

"It's so beautiful," Melody said on their way home looking up, her head on Zack's shoulder.

"And clear," Zack said. He pointed. "Look at Cassiopeia and the Milky Way. Most nights you can hardly see them. "

"I can identify the moon," Melody said, "But that's it."

"I'd be happy to show you stuff," Zack said.

"How come you know so much?"

"Think about it, Melody. I'm a pilot. I'm supposed to know."

Melody nodded. "Of course," she said.

"The first thing I'll show you is how to find Polaris." He looked up and pointed again. "All you have to do is locate the Big Dipper and from there it's easy."

He turned his head to look at her.

"It's the most important star in the sky so you need to know where it is."

"Why is it the most important?"

"Because it's better than a compass. If you can find Polaris you'll never lose your way."

"That would definitely be good to know," Melody said.

"One night soon we'll choose *our* star," he said.

"Why not now?" Melody said.

"Okay. You pick it."

"Hmm," she said. "Let's see. There are so many. Do you know all their names?"

"Probably not," Zack said.

Melody pointed. "How about that really bright one?"

"Sirius," he said. "Good pick. He put his arm around her and kissed her. It was the sweetest, gentlest kiss she'd ever received.

"Marry me," he said. "Marry me."

She wondered if he tended to say everything twice.

He kissed her again.

"Okay," Melody said.

That's what I'll tell our children if I can remember it all, Melody thought before she fell asleep.

WEDNESDAY, AUGUST 16, 2073

Sarah felt fine, her fever was down, nearly normal, and she wanted to go home. She pointed out to the doctor that the treatment of lights had worked perfectly. Her lungs were clear, and besides she only had two weeks left to live. So what if she wasn't one hundred percent cured? The doctor agreed. He was in his early eighties, and said he thought he knew how she felt, even though he didn't, because no one could, unless in her exact situation.

When Lionel arrived at the hospital for a late morning visit, Sarah was gone.

"How did she get home?" he asked the nurse on duty.

"Medivan," she said.

"Then I take it she wasn't well enough to leave on her own." His face flushed. He was angry.

"Would you like to talk to the doctor, Senator?"

"Later," he said.

Sarah had planned to go into the Memory as soon as she got home. She approached the globe and said, "On." She wanted to tell Jeff exactly how angry she was about their marriage—and especially his cheating at the very end of his life. It was unforgivable. But he probably wouldn't care and it wouldn't change anything. So, she asked herself, what was the point?

The point was that she might stop screaming at him in countless imaginary and unsatisfactory tête à têtes. She might be able to let it all go—have some peace.

She'd wash up, change her clothes and make up her mind.

When Lionel arrived to check on her, she wasn't visible. Her door was unlocked, as was everyone's on the island since there was little to steal and nobody needed anything. He saw the globe of light and knew what it must be, although he hadn't any Memory disks of his own—and that was fine, because he couldn't think of a time he cared to revisit. He approached the diaphanous, shimmering globe and hesitated. He couldn't bring himself to enter. He'd wait outside.

Sarah washed up, changed her clothes and picked up her quilting project, which was in a basket next to her bed.

I'll hem some squares, she thought. It always calmed her. *Then I'll decide.*

Sarah came out of her bedroom, said "off" to the globe of light and saw that Lionel was sitting on her terrace, his back to the door. He was a good man and obviously cared about her. Enough to help her escape and risk his reputation. She approached slowly. She was asking a lot of him.

An invitation to a suspect's home must be unusual, Krantz thought. Then while Roy Desroy was getting him coffee, Krantz began to pick up on his excitement and an idea occurred to him. *Maybe this guy has something.*

"You're not going to believe this," Roy told him. He'd said exactly the same thing last night on the omniplus.

Roy set a mug of coffee on the table next to Krantz. The wall screens that dominated most homes, as it did this one, were dark.

"Okay," Roy said, folding his arms and arranging his face in its most serious mode. "Before we begin, there's something I need to explain. I think you know I'm a robotician. But I've taken it to another level."

"That's nice," Krantz said politely. The coffee was too hot, the way he liked it.

"Okay, now hear me out. Early this year, I designed a tiny, nearly invisible robot, made a bunch of them and placed them around the island to see if they'd work."

"Uh huh," Krantz said.

"These little robots record both the sounds and sights of anything going on around them within a radius of twenty feet. They also follow the signal of a given object."

"You're kidding."

Roy shook his head. "So okay. We're in luck. You're about to see and hear everything that went on at the dock Sunday afternoon from when Tessa arrived with the bubble-glasses and I arrived a few minutes later with the intoxofloat, to right after Sarah Rally stumbled home. It's about three o'clock when it starts."

Krantz jumped up." My God, that's unbelievable!" he said with excitement while, spilling coffee on his right thigh. Then he screamed. "EEYA!";

Roy got up, went to the kitchen, came back and handed Krantz a towel. He took Krantz's cup and refilled it. Krantz wiped his pants and lowered himself slowly onto the couch.

"Okay, hold onto your hat," Roy said. He had made a composition of the videos from the various snoop-ops around the dock and the fishing hut, absent the part with Huxley and Wilbur and anything else that made him look bad.

Krantz put down his coffee and leaned forward, his pupils dilated.

"So there wasn't a murder. It was a goddamn accident," Krantz said fifty minutes later.

"You sound disappointed," Roy said.

"It's just been a damn waste of my time and everyone else's, too."

"Would you have believed the woman Tessa tried to kill if she'd told you what really happened?"

"Sarah Rally." Krantz thought for a minute. "Not sure. Probably not. The whole thing is too crazy."

"I never would have believed Tessa could turn so mean," Roy said. "It was horrible to watch."

"My superiors are going to want to see that video," Krantz said. "Those little babies are worth their weight in gold."

"They're under half an ounce apiece," Roy said.

"Never mind. Come on, bring everything. Let's go."

Pictures of Tessa were on all the wall-to-walls in all places, all day long, beginning Wednesday afternoon at one o'clock. The reporter announced, "Mystery death solved. According to Investigator Krantz of the Swyannah Police Department, it was an accident. Tessa Posnoff fell off the dock and hit her head on a bed of rocks. A video of the events leading to her death will be shown later. Thanks to Roy Desroy, head robotician at Pine Haven, and his army of snoop-ops, we know exactly what happened."

Earlier Lionel's omniplus had lit up. It was Krantz, with a rundown of everything he'd seen on the video.

"I don't believe Mrs. Rally told anyone what Tessa did," he said, after completing his lengthy review.

"I don't either," agreed Lionel.

"A brave woman. I wonder why she didn't tell me."

"Sarah's here. I'll put her on."

"Wait. You fill her in. I've got to go." Krantz was anxious to get the news to the world and get credit as soon as possible.

"All right," Lionel said.

"What's up?" Sarah said.

"This is going to blow your mind."

"I haven't heard that expression in decades."

Lionel chuckled. "I'm glad you're sitting down," he said.

Sarah listened attentively, shaking her head in disbelief. When Lionel was finished, she said, "That's extraordinary. You mean you can see and hear all that?"

"So Krantz says. He wants to know why you didn't tell anyone the whole story."

"If people had believed me," Sarah said, "Tessa would have been fired or worse—arrested, and if they hadn't— I'd have been labeled a nut. Plus it was her word against mine. Tessa would have denied it."

"If she'd been alive."

"Right, well I had no idea she wasn't. Poor Tessa."

"Come on. Poor Tessa, my eye. Poor you! Let me see those scrapes. You've certainly kept them under wraps."

"They're practically healed."

"I've been thinking that you should sue Pine Haven HEAVEN, all of HEAVEN, or both. Their employee attacked and tried to drown you, and that's got to be grounds."

"But I'm about to escape."

"Maybe you can sue for time."

"Does that mean you're getting cold feet?"

"No, it's just the lawyer in me talking. We're set for Saturday morning no matter what the weather. Prepare to drown, old girl."

Before the wall-to-wall had the story, Krantz omniplussed Zack, then Huxley, and then Melody with the news.

Roy omniplussed Annemarie. They met at a coffee shop in Swyannah, where they both ordered tea and sat in silence. Finally, Roy spoke. "Okay, Annemarie, you can avoid seeing the video, but people will be talking about it, so you need to know Tessa's death was an accident."

Annemarie sighed.

"But that's not all. She was trying to drown an elderly resident, Sarah Rally. Tessa was drunk and turned her anger on Mrs. Rally."

"You shouldn't have left Tessa in that condition."

"I've been telling myself the same thing. The truth is I wanted to get away from her. She was saying terrible things."

"I know how she could be," said Annemarie. "But still, she shouldn't have been left alone. Couldn't you have omniplussed for help?"

"Oh God," he said. "I didn't think of it."

"I've got to go," Annemarie said, getting up. "This is too painful and I need to make arrangements for Tessa's memorial service."

"When will it be?" Roy asked.

Annemarie shrugged. "Probably tomorrow."

"Maybe there's something I can do," Roy said.

Annemarie got up. "Stick to your robots," she said.

THURSDAY, AUGUST 17, 2073

Granny, I've gone and got myself engaged to the wrong man. I don't mean there's a right man, at least not yet, but Zack can't be the right one—can he? Wouldn't I be thinking and dreaming about him if he was? Wouldn't I be dying to have sex with him if he was? What should I do? Granny? Granny? Where are you? Are you listening? Okay, I get it. Tell the truth. But I hate hurting anyone's feelings and Zack, you know, is a really nice guy.

Annemarie's memorial service for her sister was supposed to take place at the Pine Haven All-Faith/No Faith Center, but because it was attended by the entire population of Pine Haven and two hundred or so residents of Swyannah arriving by boat or plane taxi, it had to be moved to the beach. Ben and the other robots were nearly overwhelmed checking them in even though they stopped taking them to the Administrators after the first twenty.

Roy spoke. His eulogy was more of an apology. If only he had told Tessa they'd get married as soon as possible. If only he had omniplussed for help, so that Tessa wasn't left by herself on the dock. He said she was a great beauty and that he'd loved her. He cried all the way through.

Lionel gave a long, poetic speech on the meaning of life. He said he had no idea what it was, but he felt Tessa had come the closest to living life to the full than anyone he'd ever known.

Annemarie said her sister was a good person, even if the video showed another side of her.

Investigator Krantz thanked Roy for his invention of the snoop-ops that had cracked the case. He predicted that Roy would become incredibly rich, now that the entire world knew of his miniscule robots. Finally, he remembered Tessa and said she had given a great many people a great deal of happiness.

Lionel suddenly remembered where he'd seen Roy before.

Ben thought death was an even odder concept than hunger, and yet it was often around him—residents, the people he guarded, disappeared suddenly. Later, he was informed they were gone, their names and identification cues removed from the computer. When he spotted Tessa, unmoving beneath the water, he recognized death, although she was the first corpse he'd ever seen. Where did the Tessa part of her go? The motor? He needed to know more or his dissertation would be nothing but a list of questions like:

What does it mean to be alive?
What does it mean to be sick?
What does it feel like to die?
What's the point of everything?

At the memorial service, Ben took notes and asked more questions: Why did so many people come to the service? They couldn't all be her friends.

Hardly anyone but Roy and Annemarie cried. People are supposed to cry at such events. *Why didn't more of them cry?* God wasn't mentioned much at the service, although there must have been many there who believed in His existence. The Pine Haven minister gave what he called a 'blessing,' and talked about the Lord Almighty and how He moved in mysterious ways." He asked people to bow their heads, which they did, and then he said a "prayer." When he finished, most people said, "Amen."

This was too big a project for one robot.

Huxley spotted Melody walking slowly ahead of him after the service. "I'll be right back, Mom," he told Harriet, and ran to catch up with Melody. "Hey," he said, "are you coming to rehearsal later?"

"Why wouldn't I?"

"I thought you might be in mourning for Tessa. I figured you were friends."

"No, she wasn't a friend," Melody said. "I'm sorry about the accident, but I can't say I feel any grief." She looked at him. "I suppose that sounds awful."

"No, Miss Melody, it's just the truth. I don't feel any either."

"But you knew Tessa pretty well," Melody said.

"Not all that well," he said. "Look at the crowd. Everyone knew Tessa. Say," he interrupted himself. "I'll see you later."

"Okay," Melody said.

Up ahead, Zack was waiting. He grinned at her.

"Zack," Melody said, as he put his arm around her waist and drew her close.

"Hey," he said.

"I don't know how to say this. It's really hard, but here's the thing. The other night was perfect, wasn't it? You know, what with the wine and the stars and everything you said to me. I mean it was really, really

163

romantic—and wonderful." She hesitated. "And I'm afraid I got carried away." She waited. No response. "The truth is—I don't know how I feel about you." She waited. "I mean I know I like you a lot but that's all I know at this point."

Zack slowly removed his arm. "I should have known it was too good to be true," he said. He shook his head. "It's my fault. I said way too much—way too soon." He shook his head again. "Sorry."

"Oh Zack, don't be sorry. It was an evening I'll never forget." Melody squeezed his arm.

"Good. Me neither."

"And we still have our star," Melody said.

"Right."

"And I still want to know how to find Polaris."

"Great. I'm your guy," Zack said. "Just let me know when."

Maybe I didn't completely blow it. Maybe there's hope after all, he thought.

Ben watched Roy carefully throughout the ceremony, and decided he must not have looked at the snoop-op videos beyond Tessa's accident and Sarah's flight, so he didn't know about Ben's arrival at the dock. At least, not yet. Ben could get into a whole lot of trouble if Roy realized Ben had seen Tessa dead in the water Sunday afternoon and didn't omniplus for help. If only he had gone right to the dock while Tessa was fighting with whoever it was, he knew he could have saved her. He would have escorted her home. Even though he thought Lionel was the man arguing with her, he should have done his duty.

After the service, Ben received a command from Roy. He was to come for an overhaul at four-thirty before he made his rounds. The more he thought about the call, the more apprehensive Ben became. Roy was going to eviscerate him. He knew it. Now it was clear Roy must have watched the video after all, which showed Ben at the dock following the accident, and he now knew what Ben had done or rather, hadn't done. He had to hide or he'd be non-existent. Perhaps he could tell Melody what was up and ask her to go to Swyannah and wait for him. He'd paddle over and she'd find a place for him to hide until he figured out what to do.

"Oowee," he called. Nothing. "OOWEE."

Finally, he heard Babe barking, the sound moving closer. In a few minutes Babe arrived followed by Melody.

"Let me think about it," Melody said, after Ben explained what he believed Roy would do to him and why. "I have an idea."

"So do I," Ben said. "I could hide out until it gets dark—then swim to Swyannah where you'd meet me."

"Mmm," Melody said. "That might work. But why don't you just meet me at the Departure Pavilion at four o'clock? We'll decide then."

At four o'clock, Ben entered beneath arches through a giant door into the central room of the Departure Pavilion, a huge room where, he supposed, Melody worked. It resembled some medical amphitheaters he'd seen in old movies, except instead of one, there were six gleaming seven-by-three-foot slabs and instead of rows of seats rising to the ceiling, there was a slim, black plane, its nose toward the enormous wall-door. Its loading dock was open and Ben could see there were people prone inside.

"I didn't hear you come in," Melody said, from inside the plane. "I'm just fastening the Finals into position so they don't shift during flight."

"We don't have much time," said Ben. "I turned off my connection to Roy and the other robots just before I passed the dining hall. As soon as he notices, he'll come looking for me."

"Don't worry," Melody said. "You'll be gone by then."

"Great," Ben said. "How?"

"Can't you guess?" Melody asked, jumping down from the cabin. "Look. There's just enough room in the center aisle for a twelve-foot crocodile."

"Oh," Ben said. "But I've never flown before."

"You'll love it," Melody said. She pulled down the ramp. "Easy as pie," she said. "Crawl in."

Ben hesitated. "What about those people?"

"They used to be people," Melody told him. "Now they're Finals."

"Corpses?" Ben said.

"They won't bother you. They won't bother anyone ever again."

"I don't like it. Couldn't we go with my original idea? I'll swim to Swyannah and meet you."

"Ben," Melody said. "Get in."

Slowly, he approached the ramp. More slowly, he crawled up and settled himself on the floor between the permanent gurneys, three to a side.

"Is my tail all in?" Ben asked.

"Yes."

"This is suffocating."

"Download something," Melody said.

"Not in the mode," Ben said.

"Very funny," said Melody. "As soon as Zack gets here, you'll be off."

"Does he know I'm in here?"

"Not yet."

"What if he doesn't like it?"

"He will," Melody said.

"Where am I going?"

"Never mind. You'll be safe, and that's what's important."

"When will I see you?" Ben asked.

"Soon," Melody said. "Maybe tomorrow."

Ben made a plaintive noise.

"Ben," Melody said, "stop. You're driving me crazy."

She closed the door of the aerohearse and waited for Zack.

Four-thirty-five and Ben hadn't arrived. Roy checked their connection. Dead. It might not mean anything, although it had never, to his knowledge, happened before. He waited a few more minutes until it was clear Ben wasn't coming. He notified the six other robots to look for him. "Something's wrong with the big guy," he said. "I think he needs help."

The snoop-op videos had shown Ben by the dock, but it wasn't clear what he'd seen. The time showed him there after the murder, but he could have arrived earlier—Roy couldn't be certain. The snoop-ops might have missed him, and he wasn't going to take a chance. Five minutes was all he needed to remove Ben's recent memory. Ben would never know the difference. The worrisome thing was that Ben seemed to be on the run, which, if so, meant he was afraid.

According to Grot, the second-in-command, Ben had been sighted near the Pavilion shortly before four o'clock.

"Okay—then find Melody," Roy instructed. "Maybe he stopped by to see her."

"Not a problem," Grot said. He connected back after a minute. "I have her location. According to the third-in-command, she's heading toward the launch."

"Good. I'm not far away."

"What happened to Ben?" Grot asked.

"I'll know more later," Roy said, "but I think he's had a breakdown. He hasn't been coming in for regular check-ups."

"What should I tell the others?"

"Nothing yet," Roy said. He was coming up on Melody. They hadn't spoken since he had dropped her. "Hey, good-looking," he said.

Melody turned around. She didn't smile. "I was at the memorial service. Sorry about Tessa," she said.

"Thanks," Roy said. "She was a good woman, you know."

"She tried to kill Sarah," Melody said.

"Yes, you always liked Sarah," Roy said.

"That's not what I meant. I meant—good people don't attempt murder," Melody said.

"Okay," Roy said. "Got it. Say, have you seen Ben in the last hour?"

Melody paused. "No, the last time was at Tessa's memorial."

"Well, let me know if you run into him. He needs help."

In the minutes it took to fly to underground storage, Ben had started to explain to Zack why he thought Roy wanted to eviscerate him. When they landed, Zack said, "Hold on—I need to take care of the Finals and then it'll be your turn."

"Turn for what?" Ben asked.

"See those shelves?"

Ben had backed out of the plane so Zack could reach the bodies. Zack pointed. "I'm going to hide you on one of them."

"Please don't," Ben pleaded.

"Come on, Ben," Zack said. "You'll be one hundred percent safe. Isn't that what you want?"

"Mmmhmm," Ben said.

"Good." Zack leaned down and patted Ben's head. "Don't forget, before I leave, I want to hear the rest of your story."

"Okay," Ben said. He pointed at the machine onto which Zack was loading the Finals. "Are you going to use that thing to get me up on a shelf?"

"It's called an eleva-wheel ," Zack said, "and yes, I'll need to use it."

"Just so long as I'm face-forward. I want to see what's going on."

Zack laughed. "Don't worry. You'll have a perfect view," he said.

Melody's face appeared on Zack's omniplus. "What's up?" he asked her.

"Roy is looking for Ben."

"I'd sure like to know why."

"Hasn't Ben told you?

"He's about to," Zack said.

Lionel settled himself down to write notes on the mystery of Pine Haven.

Woman found dead in river. Blow or blows to back of head. Accident or murder? It appears to be an accident. Unless some of the now-cleared suspects were lying—I lied, for example. What if Roy lied about coming back to the dock? He must have come back or I wouldn't have seen him half dripping-wet on my way back to the hospital. Got to prove he lied. Got to talk to Zack. Now.

"Yeah I think there's more to this Roy/Ben situation than we know," Zack said, when Lionel's face and story came through on his omniplus. "Ben thinks it's all about his seeing Tessa in the river and not reporting her death."

"I think it may be more than that," Lionel said.

"Ben was protecting you. Did you know that?"

"Me?" Lionel asked.

"He overheard an argument between Tessa and someone else. He wasn't sure, but he thought the other person might be you. And then," he continued, "he saw you on the path not far from the dock.

"I didn't see him," Lionel said.

"Obviously."

"Too bad we don't know what was said."

"We do," Zack said. "Ben has a recording."

"You're kidding! I'll be right over," Lionel said.

"No, I'll come get you. I'm with Ben at the StrataDrome outside Swyannah."

"Okay, I'll walk to the strip."

"Do you know what Roy's timeline was?" Lionel asked as he settled in the aerohearse next to Zack.

"What are you talking about?"

"The afternoon of Tessa's accident."

"Oh. Hmm. I don't remember the exact time, but he said he left Tessa at the dock and went to his apartment before flying to Darby."

"Which way?"

"By the small bridge."

"You're sure he didn't return to the dock?"

"Not according to Roy," Zack said.

Halfway through rehearsal, Melody saw Lionel on her omniplus. "Excuse me. I'll just be a minute," she said to Huxley.

"Zack and I just listened to a recording of Tessa's conversation with Huxley the afternoon she died," Lionel said.

"With Huxley? My God," Melody said. "How is that possible?"

"I'll explain later. The point is—we need to talk to him. Ask him to come over here after rehearsal. Okay?"

"Yes, absolutely," Melody said. She felt dizzy. "Where are you?"

"At the StrataDrome with Ben," said Lionel. "We're both spooked."

"What's up?" Huxley asked.

"After rehearsal, we've got to talk."

"Right now you need to sit down," Huxley said. He pushed a stool toward her.

"Thanks. Just for a minute." Melody said.

When Melody and Huxley emerged from the back exit of the Come and Get It Café, they walked one short block down to a dusty lot filled with rows of mostly ancient bicycles, where Huxley kept his glorious new model, a blazing red Bullitt, under lock and key. He spoke to a man in the hut. "Got a rental for my friend here?" he asked. "Something cool with a slot, front and center, for her omniplus."

Melody and Huxley cycled toward the StrataDrome while Lionel, via omniplus, told them what he, Zack and Ben now knew.

"Huxley," Lionel began, Zack and I heard exactly what you, and Tessa said to each other the afternoon of the accident. If it was an accident," Lionel added ominously.

"Wait a minute. How did you hear that?" Melody asked.

"Ben has a recording," Lionel said.

"Really?" Melody said. "I don't get it."

"We'll explain later," Lionel said, annoyed. "Now if you'll just let me continue. After listening, the only thing we can say for sure is that you, Huxley, didn't have anything to do with it."

'What do you mean by *it*?" Huxley asked.

"Tessa's death." *What else could it be?* Lionel thought.

'How can you be sure?" Huxley asked.

"Okay, it's not for sure but it's a strong hunch," Lionel said. *What's his problem? Does he want me to think he's guilty?*

"I'm here, too, guys," Zack interjected. He was standing next to Lionel with Ben. "Okay, here's something we *can* say for sure, Huxley. Roy must have come back for Wilbur just as Tessa told you he would."

"How do you know that?" Huxley asked.

"Annemarie and I saw the little fellow when we were in Darby. He was with Roy," Zack said.

"I'm confused. Who is the little fellow? Melody asked.

"Wilbur. His baby robot," Zack said.

Lionel jumped in. "Which means Roy lied to Krantz and could have killed Tessa," he said. "And here's something I just told Zack. I saw Roy dripping-wet that afternoon on his way back, I guess, to his laboratory."

"Can you prove it?" Melody asked.

"Maybe not, but Ben said he saw me hiding near the path, probably about the same time I saw Roy."

"Why didn't you say so before?" Huxley asked.

"I didn't think it was important, and besides, I didn't know who Roy was until the memorial service. Also, I didn't want to tell Krantz I had lied. He already had me in his sights for some other errors in judgment."

"What a mess," Melody said. "It could have been cleared up if you all hadn't been so afraid of the truth."

"Not afraid," Lionel said, "just wary. Do you always tell the truth?"

"If I know what it is," Melody said. "Which, mostly, I don't."

They were approaching the site. As they rode down, braking hard all the way to the black opening, Huxley said, "I've got the chills. What is this place?" he asked.

"It's where we bring the Finals. I guess it's a little spooky till you're used to it," Melody said.

"Are you used to it?

"Not sure," Melody said. "That is to say, no."

Everyone listened hard to Ben's recording. The confirmation of Huxley and Tessa's once-intimate relationship was unpleasant for Melody to hear, and she couldn't stop thinking about it. Maybe intimate wasn't the right word, since it implied exclusivity, didn't it? Intimacy, after all, wasn't just physical. She noted Huxley's face showed a blotchy redness she'd never seen before. Maybe it was a sign of embarrassment and if so, she was glad. It showed he knew she knew he'd lied about being close to Tessa. At least he had a conscience, which she doubted Roy ever did—especially now that it appeared he may have killed Tessa.

"Poor woman," she said aloud, without meaning to.

Lionel, Zack and Huxley nodded in agreement.

They were all too focused on the recording to hear or notice Krantz. He had left his cart up the road and walked down to the cave. He peered inside, squinted at the four standing or sitting in the dim light of the facility and then followed their gazes up to where Ben was holding court on his shelf. His mouth dropped two chin levels.

"What the hell is this?" he asked, his voice cracking like an adolescent's. "Jesus." He paused. "Christ Jesus. Jesus Christ."

"Shh," Melody admonished him, wondering how he'd found his way to them and why he was there.

"Sorry," Krantz said, "but I can't believe what I think I see."

"They're Finals," Melody said. "Thousands of them, preserved and perfect forever."

"I don't like it," Krantz said. "I really, really don't like it. And I can't imagine it's legal."

"The United States Congress says it is," Lionel said.

Krantz heard Tessa's voice on the recording. "Am I hearing who I think I'm hearing?" he said. "Or am I losing my mind?"

"It's Tessa," Huxley said. "If you'd be quiet a minute, Ben will start it over so you can hear the whole sequence."

"Of what?" asked Krantz.

"Of Tessa and me when I passed by the dock," said Huxley.

"The day of the accident?" Krantz asked.

"The day of the murder," Lionel corrected, deepening the last word. "Here, take a seat." He pointed to a long bench where Huxley sat, holding his head.

"Thanks," Krantz said. He nudged Huxley. "Did you say, Ben?"

"Uh huh," Huxley said.

"The robot?" asked Krantz.

"Uh huh," Huxley said.

"Of Pine Island?" Krantz asked.

"Uh huh," Huxley said. "Hey, who's there?" he inquired of some approaching footsteps.

"Well then," Krantz said, "I'm afraid I have to arrest someone here for the crime of abduction and then return Ben to his rightful owner."

"That would be me," said a voice from the entrance. It was Roy's.

Roy had watched Melody leave Pine Haven. He had a gut feeling she knew more about Ben's disappearance than she'd let on. He decided to make a visit to Krantz, who was now something of a buddy. He had omniplussed him and explained that Ben, his top robot, had been stolen, and he thought it was possible he'd been taken to the mainland. "I'd sure appreciate your help," he said.

"You've got it," Krantz said. "I suppose you looked all over the island."

"Yes," Roy said, "and my remaining six robots will keep on looking."

"I'll get my cart and meet you at the landing," he said. Krantz and other law enforcement agents were allowed to drive small carts in Swyannah, as long as it was case-related.

"One more thing," Roy said. "I've got a hunch that Melody might have a part in this."

"Okay," Krantz said. "We'll check her out."

"How does someone steal a robot?" he asked Roy later, when they were driving around the city in what Roy felt was slow motion.

"I've been trying to figure that out myself," Roy said.

"Maybe he ran away," Krantz speculated.

"Why would he do that?"

"I'm joking. Of course, it's out of the question." Krantz parked outside the Come and Get It Café. "My deputy tells me this is where Melody rehearses with Huxley's band on Thursdays."

"I hadn't heard."

"You must know she can sing," Krantz said.

"We never discussed it," Roy said.

"Didn't she sing when you were together?"

"I don't remember," Roy said.

"Okay," Krantz said. "There's a back entrance to this joint. I think we'll just sit there in the shade if we can find some, and wait till they come out."

"Then what?" Roy asked.

"Follow them," Krantz said.

Melody gasped. "Roy!"

"You didn't think I was smart enough to find Ben, did you?" Roy said, a satisfied expression on his face. "Well, thanks to you, I did—Wilbur and I, that is." He took the little robot out, put it on a shelf and gloated.

Lionel stood between Roy and the shelf that was bearing Ben. "There's no way you're going to get hold of Ben. He'll be state's evidence in your trial," Lionel said to Roy. "Krantz here will have proprietary rights."

"Hold on," Krantz growled. "What evidence? What trial?"

"Sit down," Lionel said. "We've lots to tell you."

"This is shit," Roy shouted. "I'm leaving."

"You just got here," Zack said, blocking the exit.

"What makes you think Tessa's death wasn't an accident?" Krantz asked Lionel.

"Ask Huxley."

"Okay. Huxley, what makes…"

"I heard you—and I believe you just heard Tessa say Roy had left Wilbur behind by accident."

"So?" Krantz asked.

"It meant, according to Tessa, that Roy would definitely come back to get him," Huxley explained. "However according to Roy, he never went back."

"But you think he did?" Krantz said.

"I know he did," Huxley said. "And there's the proof." He pointed to Wilbur, who was softly playing his music near Roy. "Wilbur, himself!"

"I've got a hundred Wilburs," Roy said. "You can't tell them apart. It doesn't matter if I lose one."

"There's only one thing to do," Krantz said. "We've got to see what happened after Tessa fell off the dock and landed on her back."

"I showed you everything," Roy said.

"Everything that happened before, but nothing that happened afterwards," Krantz said.

"Nothing happened afterwards," Roy said.

"Fine," Krantz said, "maybe not. Still, we're going to look and you're going to show us the works."

"I'd better do that," Ben interrupted. "Roy will erase everything if he gets a chance."

"Who do you think you are?" Roy asked, with a sharp look at Ben. "You're my creation—nothing but a goddamn machine. I was there for you. Don't you remember?"

"I remember," Ben said. "You were a nice guy. It's not my fault you changed."

"A robot is always loyal to its creator," Roy said. "That's the rule."

"Ben has evolved," Lionel said, suddenly aware that's what must have happened, "and you made it possible for him to have the opportunity. You've only yourself to blame."

"Damn it all," Roy said. "You sound like my mother. Why should I blame myself? If what you say is true, I'm a goddamn genius. Listen, evolved or not, Ben belongs to me, body and soul. It's in my contract."

"Hmmm," Melody said. "Sounds like Ben's rights were overlooked. I think he needs a good lawyer."

"I'm the one who might need a lawyer," Roy said.

"Count on it," Zack said.

Zack flew Ben, Krantz, Lionel, and Roy to the island in the limohearse. Melody and Huxley rode their bicycles back to Swyannah, accompanied at a distance by Krantz's deputies, who were dispatched to drive the cart.

"Is it true about you and Roy?" Huxley asked Melody after they'd mounted their bikes and toiled up the hill from the cave.

"Afraid so," Melody said.

"You couldn't tell what kind of a guy he was?" Huxley asked, looking over.

Her face was red.

"No, I thought he was the real thing," Melody said.

"What's that?" Huxley asked.

"For starters, someone who means what he says," Melody said.

"What else?"

"Someone who cares," Melody said. "Someone you can count on."

"It doesn't sound like such a tall order," Huxley said.

"Then why haven't you settled down?"

"Guess I've been having too much fun," Huxley said.

"With women like Tessa?" Melody asked.

"Maybe. But I'm no longer the person I was."

"Okay. Who are you now?"

"Don't know," Huxley said. "All I know is I've changed."

"No longer out for just fun and games?" Melody asked, quoting what he'd said to Tessa, and giving him a sidelong glance.

Huxley didn't answer. There was a long pause.

"Who told you about Roy and me?" Melody asked.

"Krantz let it slip when he was talking about the case the other day. He made it clear he didn't think I murdered Tessa and he thought maybe Roy did."

They both became quiet. It wasn't till after they'd returned their bikes to the lot and headed for the skimplane launch that Huxley spoke.

"Is that what you want? Settle down? Have a family and all that?"

"My first dream is to sing the songs I write."

Huxley smiled at her. "I haven't heard any of your songs."

"I didn't think you'd be interested," Melody said.

"Well, I am," Huxley said. "I want to hear them as soon as they put Mr. Roy Desroy behind bars."

"I can't wait to see what the snoop-ops saw," Melody said.

"Right," Huxley said. He took Melody's arm and helped her onto the skimplane. "You smell like lilies," he said.

Sarah was nervous. She hadn't heard from Lionel for hours and she wanted—needed—details. How was she getting off the island? Where was he taking her? How was she going to manage when she got there? When should she give him her diamonds? Could she take anything with her? It was all in his hands and since Jeff died she had become accustomed to making her own plans and decisions. Not that there'd been much to plan or decide and she hadn't even decided whether or not to give Jeff a piece of her mind in the Memory.

I have to reach Lionel...right now. In seconds Lionel's face was frowning from her omniplus.

"Hey, Sarah," he said. "Sorry, old girl, but I can't talk now. Lots happening. Later."

She didn't like him calling her old girl and she didn't like him saying later instead of goodbye. *When did he start talking like that? Never mind.* She omniplussed the Prolocutor.

Zack landed the aerohearse and left it on the airstrip. He would park it later in the Pavilion.

They were met by six robot crocodiles that immediately surrounded Roy as he exited, and escorted him toward his heliozoomer.

What the hell?" Krantz shouted, following at a respectful distance. He tapped Lionel on the shoulder and whispered, "Are you sure those crocodiles aren't real?"

"I'm sure, but they're still dangerous," Lionel said. "They were designed to be guards. Ask Ben."

"Where is he?" Melody asked. Ben had disappeared.

"Goodbye," Roy called to Krantz and the others. "I'm leaving. I'll see you when I'm good and ready." He was half into the helioozoomer opening when he screamed and fell back. Something had gripped his legs and pulled him to the ground and was dragging him through the path made by the other crocodiles, parting like a dark green sea. It was Ben.

"Help! Stop him," Roy called to Grot.

"We can't," Grot said "You gave him control of us. Remember?"

"Thank God for that," Krantz said. "Where are my deputies? They were supposed to meet us here, not those damn crocodiles."

"Over here," one deputy called out. He peered out from behind a pine tree. "We tried shooting them but it made them mad so they came after us, and if you hadn't landed, I guess they'd have shaken us down out of the tree."

"You were hiding up that tree?" Krantz was ashamed and furious. "From robots? You idiots, don't you know they're not real?"

"What? How were we supposed to know that? No one told us."

"Never mind. See the guy on the ground?"

"Uh huh," the deputies said.

"Handcuff him." Krantz looked thoughtful. "Come to think of it, put ankle cuffs on him, too. He's not going to get another chance to get away."

"Don't have any ankle cuffs. I'll have to go back to town for some."

It took thirty minutes for the deputy to return and another ten to sort the party out—first, the six subordinate crocodiles in single file—next, Roy in chains attended by two deputies and supervised by Krantz—and finally, in the rear, Ben, Lionel and Zack. When they arrived at the dock, Huxley and Melody were waiting.

"Should I ask for an explanation," Huxley said, "or just wait for wall-to-wall news?"

"Asshole," Krantz said under his breath.

"Okay, everyone," Lionel said. "Let's get cracking. We need to find the snoop-ops on the side of the dock where Tessa died."

"Right," Zack said, and with Ben's help, he and Lionel were able to locate and collect over twenty-two nearly invisible snoop-ops in and around the dock. He dropped them one by one into his flight bag.

"Will they be all right?" Melody wondered. "Won't they get crushed?"

"They're indestructible," Roy announced with pride.

"Now what?" Zack asked. "There must be a secret to seeing what those little guys recorded."

Everyone looked at Roy, who responded by smirking. "Who knows?" he said.

"Okay," Ben said. "As it happens, I do. Anyone have an omniplus?"

Everyone did.

"Turn the receptor to omicron epsilon tau twice and press up," Ben ordered.

Everyone did.

"Press up again."

They did.

"Now gamma gamma delta twice and press down."

They did.

"Hit blue once, purple twice and orange three times."

They did.

"Okay, now I need to remove the choral password. I doubt he's had time to change it since this morning." Ben's omniplus was embedded so his compbrain could activate the notes of the password command function. The first eight bars of *Hail Britannia* played followed by the bridge *of Hey Hey Hey Baby Baby Baby.*

"Ha! It worked." Ben did a little side-to-side jig. "Now let's look at the snoop-ops. If each of you checks one, it won't take long to find what we want." Ben did a little side-to-side jig.

Zack held out his flight bag. Melody, Huxley, Lionel, Krantz and he each reached in and pulled one out. Within minutes, there were shouts.

"I've got him. He's kneeling beside Tessa," Huxley said.

"I've got him, too," Lionel said. "He's walking toward her."

"All right," Krantz said. "Let's everyone watch the same one at the same time."

The snoop-op videos were out of order and from many angles, but they chose one, then others, and saw everything—Roy's return to the dock, the murder of Tessa and the salvaging of Wilbur.

"She asked Roy to help her," Melody said, "and he just went ahead and killed her. Horrible. I'll never be able to get any of it out of my mind."

"Roy," Krantz said, "you're under arrest. Remember, anything you say can be used against you."

Roy shrugged. "I know that. You can talk to my lawyer, once I'm out of these goddamn handcuffs and can omniplus."

The deputies escorted Roy to the skimplane with Krantz, Lionel and Zack following. Ben stayed to talk to the other six robots, which were in a state of confusion and murmuring among themselves.

"I'm sorry about this," Ben said to the robots, "but don't worry. The Administration will hire someone to take Roy's place. It won't be the same, but the fact is, Roy isn't the person we thought he was. Maybe he was a nice guy once, but if so, he's changed. People aren't like robots, you know."

"Yeah, but you've changed, too," Grot observed

Ben said. "Is that right? If so I can't explain it. Okay, enough. Get back to your stations."

Melody was taking Huxley on a short cut to the landing where he would wait for the next skimplane.

"It's on my way," she said when he thanked her. "I'll see you tomorrow night," she said.

"But wait—when will I hear your songs?" he asked.

"I don't know," Melody said.

"You could sing one now," Huxley said.

"Sorry," Melody said. "I've got to go home."

"Then when?" Huxley said.

"Hmm," Melody said. "How about tomorrow—after the show?"

"Sounds good," Huxley said just as Ben appeared on the side of the path.

"Keep me posted," Ben said.

"What about?" Huxley said.

"Anything. Everything. Just stay in touch."

Huxley laughed. "Not a problem," he said.

"Excellent," said Ben. "Come on, Melody. You must be tired."

To no one's surprise, once back in Swyannah, Roy was incarcerated without bail pending indictment and trial.

"Don't you understand? Tessa murdered Wilbur!" Roy protested from behind bars.

"But you resuscitated him," Huxley said.

"I didn't know I'd find his parts and be able to put him back together," Roy said. "What she did was unforgivable."

"How about what you did to her?" Zack asked.

Roy was silent.

"Don't tell my mother," Roy said.

"It's already hit the news," Zack said.

"She doesn't watch anything but Sad Story Time and The Daily Lottery," Roy said. "But sooner or later, someone will spill the beans."

"Poor woman," Zack said.

"It'll kill her," Roy said.

The Prolocutor was in a meeting when Sarah omniplussed the first time, having lunch the second and interviewing a prospective employee the third.

Persistence had been Sarah's strong suit in the work world and so, undeterred, she walked to the Administration building.

"Do you have an appointment?" the secretary asked.

"No."

"Well let's see—um—she's very busy but I could squeeze you in on September first at ten."

"Oh dear, Sarah said, "by then I'll have been dead three days."

"Did you say dead?" asked the young man.

"I did."

"Could I ask how you know that?"

"Certainly. Because HEAVEN intends to execute me on August twenty-eighth."

He paled. Clearly this sort of encounter was not part of his job description and no words were forthcoming.

"All I want is to ask the Prolocutor a quick question," Sarah said. "Don't you suppose she could find two minutes to answer it?"

"What's the question?"

"Who whittled the replica of Pine Haven at the library?"

He wrote it down. "Okay. I'll ask her when she's finished and give you a call."

"I'd rather wait," Sarah said.

Lionel was sprawled in a chaise in front of his house. "Sarah," he said, arising with some difficulty. She had rarely visited him; he always visited her.

"Don't get up," Sarah said when he already had.

"Sit here," he said, unfolding a chair. She sat.

"Excuse my appearance," he said, and lay down again. "I need a shower and a fizz before I feel human. It's been quite a day."

"Tell me about it."

"I will but I need to catch my breath first and it'll take a while to tell. Suffice it to say Roy murdered Tessa and is now behind bars."

"I'm speechless," Sarah said.

"Yeah, well so are we all."

"My God. You mean it wasn't an accident?'

"No ma'am."

"You're sure?"

"Positive."

"I can't wait to hear."

"I thought you wanted the details of your escape."

"That too."

"I won't know until tomorrow afternoon after I get everything set."

"You'd better take my diamonds with you."

"What for?"

"To pay for things. You know."

"Sarah, the truth is I don't need your damn diamonds. You'll be fine. Trust me."

How she hated that phrase. "Okay," she said.

"Give them to your kids."

"They don't need them either."

"I'm sure you know someone who does."

Sarah rose. "Maybe," she said.

Zack had been surprised to hear from Sarah and even more surprised to learn she knew he whittled.

"My dad taught me," he said in answer to her question. He added, "It passes the time while I'm waiting. I do a lot of that."

Her face beamed at him from the omniplus. "I wonder if you have any idea how talented you are, Zack. That replica of Pine Haven is awesome."

"Thank you."

"You're welcome."

"How did you find out I was the one who made it?"

"I dragged it out of the Prolocuter. Do you mind?"

"No, it's okay."

"Good. I'm glad. Now—if you have a minute, I've got a proposition for you."

"Sure. Shoot."

"A number of years ago, my husband started a movement called *Hands on Forever.*"

"Never heard of it, "Zack said.

"That's the problem. Not many have. It's a program to encourage people to use their hands to do things—make things."

"I see." Zack said although he didn't.

Jeff believed people's brains would change for the worse if they didn't.

"Okay."

"I thought you might be willing to take it over when I'm gone," she continued.

Zack couldn't think of what to say.

"There used to be whittling festivals in this country but they've disappeared. Maybe you could bring them back."

"Me? I've never organized anything. I'm more or less a loner."

Sarah ignored him. "Otherwise it's pretty much a lost art."

"I can't be the only whittler in the world."

"Probably not," Sarah said, "but do you know any others?"

"No," Zack said.

"You could do something about that."

"How?"

"Give virtual classes on the LimitLessLink."

"Come on."

"People would pay to learn. You'd have fun, make money and at the same time teach people one great way to use their hands."

Zack grunted. *Crazy*, he thought.

"I'll give you the capital to get it going."

"Why?"

"It's important."

"To you?"

"Well, yes to me—but more than that—I think Jeff was right and it's important for people to use their hands in a creative way and, frankly, I'd like to be part of something worthwhile."

"I don't know. It's a tall order but—okay."

"You'll do it?"

"No, I meant okay, I'll think about it."

"I need to know," Sarah said. Her face faded from the screen and then reappeared. "Soon," she added.

FRIDAY, AUGUST 18, 2073

Roy was wrong. Not only didn't Mrs. Burch die, she was, for once, watching the news on her outdoor screen when she learned of his arrest the next morning. She fell off her sofa-swing, landed on her left side on the concrete floor of her porch, then rolled onto her back, where she lay flailing the air like a large helpless bug.

"I've got to see my boy," she said to the reporters who soon discovered her. "I know they forced a confession out of him. He would never do such a thing. Never."

"You suppose they'll let Roy come see me before I die?" she asked a hospital aide after she'd been brought by ambulance to the hospital, examined and attached to the latest machines to monitor her life signs while she enjoyed a certain celebrity status as Mother of Roy Desroy. "It won't be long. My poor heart's ready to burst."

"Your heart's all right," said the aide, a young muscular man with an air of authority. "I'm looking at your vitals on the screen. Nothing wrong with you from what I see, but you need to check with your doctor. If I'm correct, you can go see him as soon as you like."

"Praise the Lord," said Mrs. Burch. "I'll just borrow my brother's trailer and be on the way to see my sweet boy."

The aide looked doubtful.

"Don't worry, my nieces will help me. They always do so I'm almost never alone—except I was when I fell off the swing," Mrs. Burch said.

"Your nieces must be strong," the aide observed.

"That's an impudent remark, sonny. Bet your mama would be ashamed of you," Mrs. Burch said. "Never mind. I'll overlook it if you'll just run and find my nieces. They'll be sitting in the waiting room, side by side, dressed alike, reading *Horrible but True* or *Disgusting Crimes*, even if they're old issues. They're celebrity and murder-obsessed. You can't miss them. They're twins."

"Okay, I'll be right back," he said to Mrs. Burch.

The girls were waiting exactly as described by their aunt. The aide said their aunt was going on a trip and wanted them to go with her.

"Where's she going?"

"Swyannah," the aide said.

The girls jumped up and ran down the corridor to Mrs. Burch's room.

"Oh my God, oh my God," the girls squealed. "Is this a dream come true or what?"

"If you lose your job because of this, don't worry," said Lionel as Hoppy left the coast of Maine.

"I'm not worried," said Zack.

"Sure you are."

"No, I'm really not."

"Well, if it happens I'll find you something else."

"Okay," Zack said. "Thanks." He grinned at Lionel. "I'm happy to help. Sarah's a great lady if a little pushy and I'm glad she's not going to Depart. Melody would be glad too, though of course she won't know what happened."

"What did you think of my place?"

"Uh..."

"You didn't like it."

"No, I liked it fine but I don't think Sarah will."

"It's temporary."

"Right."

"And it's comfortable. I know because I used to stay there a lot when I was younger and wanted to get away."

"Right."

"It's got everything anyone could want."

"Except a view and fresh air."

"Come on. It has great views through the screen-alls and sea air is piped in constantly. There's even a revolving telescope. I forgot to show it to you. You can look at the stars."

"Right."

"The kind of house Sarah wants is no longer available. Those old clapboard houses are museums now, owned and operated by the State. Don't fret. I'll find something she'll like but it'll take more than a day."

Hoppy was approaching Pine Haven's landing strip.

"Hey Zack, thanks for your help," Lionel said.

"Save that for when Sarah's safe and sound in your— what do you call it?"

"Cave," Lionel said.

Hey Granny. Good news. Huxley said he really likes my songs—really, really likes them. He says he really, really likes me too. I told him I thought he was always making fun of me, the way he smiled in such a sarcastic way and called me Miss Melody. Huxley was surprised. "I always liked you," he said. "Always, and now I like you even more." Now I was the surprised one. "You're kidding. Boy, you sure fooled me," I said. Then he moved close, put his arms around me. As he did he said, "Miss Melody, maybe you and I should go to the capital of song together. We could collaborate."

While I was taking that in, Granny, he hauled off and kissed me. I have to admit it was right up there on the charts of the best kisses of my lifetime, so if I remember correctly, I kissed him back. It all lasted a long time, so it's hard to say what was going on, since I nearly passed out. Are you laughing, Granny? Well, stop. I know you think it's too soon to get serious about anyone. It's true I was crazy for Roy, and carried a torch for him until I fell for Lionel, then I sort of got engaged to Zack and now it's Huxley. It doesn't sound emotionally possible, but don't forget, I never kissed Lionel and the kiss Zack gave me was cousinly at most, so when you think about it, it's been three months since I had a bona-fide smooch. Right? I mean after three months, it's okay to be in love again—isn't it? Granny? Any thoughts? I'd ask you for a sign but the one you sent last time didn't work out too well, so I'll just go with my, God help me, instincts.

Lionel fell onto Sarah's lounge chair and lay there eyes closed.

"Was that a moan?" Sarah asked.

"No, just a sigh. But never mind, we're all set for tomorrow."

"Great. Tell me everything."

Lionel sat up. "First of all you need to know Zack is in the picture.

"Okay."

"He won't tell anyone and he's happy to help."

"Okay."

"I can't pull it off by myself."

"I *get* it."

"Also it involves a disguise."

"That's so dorky. Who's going to wear it?"

"You."

Sarah covered her face with her hands.

"Was that a moan?" Lionel asked.

"Yes," Sarah said.

"It gets worse," Lionel continued. "You're going to be a fish."

"What kind of fish?"

"You'll see."

"I'll tell you the rest later. I've got to go into Swyannah to pick up the disguise."

"They have fish disguises in Swyannah?"

"No it's arriving there by Swiftee. I'll show it to you when I get back." He was walking toward the airstrip.

"But--t"

"Not to fret. I promise to tell you everything you need to know then."

"Need to know? What does that mean? I need to know everything."

Lionel waved and blew her a kiss.

SATURDAY, AUGUST 19, 2073

"A crime of passion," Mrs. Burch said to the lawyer Roy had her hire to defend him. A *puny-looking fellow*, she thought. *Maybe not too bright.* He was sitting across from her and the twins in her brother's mobile home, now parked outside of town in a rented field. "Isn't that what this was?"

"I'm not sure what you mean," the lawyer said.

"Roy was enraged by the murder of Wilbur. He couldn't control himself."

The twins nodded in agreement. "That's a fact," one said.

"Roy's always had a terrible temper," the other said.

"But Wilbur's a robot," the lawyer said.

"So what? Roy loved him." Mrs. Burch took a deep breath. "In any case, it wasn't premeditated."

It was hot; the twins fanned her with *Madman Murders*.

"True," the lawyer said. "I thought of that."

"Well, praise the Lord." Mrs. Burch was pink and moist with indignation and the effort of remaining cordial. "Now all you need to do is have a thought about it being a crime of passion."

"That's the ticket," the twins said in unison.

"I want my son free," Mrs. Burch said, raising her right arm high to punch the air, her fist clenched as if it held a torch.

"He's not going to be free, ma'am," the lawyer told her. "Not right away. He killed someone."

Mrs. Burch lowered her arm, nearly out of breath from the exertion. "Whose side are you on?" she asked between puffs.

"Ma'am, I'll do my utmost to have your son acquitted, and, barring that, get him a light sentence," the lawyer said. "I can do no more." He took a deep breath. "The problem is—he's on visuals murdering Tessa Posnoff in cold blood."

"Hot blood," Mrs. Burch corrected him. "Boiling hot blood, sonny. Makes all the difference in Darby."

"The trial's in Swyannah," a twin reminded her.

"Don't make no difference, Miss Smarty-pants," Mrs. Burch said, frowning. "The folks are as alike in both places as one patch of corn is to another. You ought to know that. Same good seed."

Roy was indicted and his trial set for the second week in September. Meanwhile, the twins were set to walk around town with bullhorns and signs: FREE ROY! HE'S A GOOD OL' BOY!

Late morning when the Celebration was in full swing Lionel took Sarah by the hand and led her to the beach. "It's time," he said. "Are you set?"

"I hope so. Let's review. We're racing our slitherboats."

"Right."

"I move ahead." Sarah looked at Lionel. Will people believe that's possible?"

"They'll believe I want you to win. It's your Celebration and your last race so you have to win."

"Okay. When I'm near the peninsula—I capsize the boat."

"Right."

"Then I slip into my shark suit."

"Right."

"Which is already in the boat."

"Right."

"I snorkel to shore with only the fin showing."

"Right."

"I hope I can do that."

"You can—there's an automatic eterna-cell motor inside the suit. Once you start it up it will keep going till you turn it off. I showed you how it worked. It's easy. Remember?"

"Right. Zack will be waiting for me in the bushes at end of the peninsula."

"Right."

"He'll help me out of the water and hide me in the back of his Sardinia. Then we'll drive to wherever it is he's hidden Hoppy."

"Right."

"And off we'll go."

"Right."

"Then you'll come see me after the search for my body is called off."

"Perfect."

"And we'll talk about what happens from there."

"Exactly."

"Okay, I'm ready. Let's go."

For the days previous, the Pine Haven administration considered how to compensate Sarah for the attack and the forbearance she exhibited by keeping the incident to herself. Even after the video of her attempted murder was seen everywhere, she was so circumspect with the media that the story died as rapidly as she was scheduled to do on August twenty-eighth. Even if they postponed her

Departure, it was clear that when her time came, the public would focus on the attack again and the fallout might be damaging. The program, after all, emphasized a decade of carefree living in a secure environment without the threat of death before the appropriate time.

They had sent their deliberations to Washington, whereupon the HEAVEN commission met, reviewed all the particulars, and voted to lobby Congress to create a special, one-time award to Sarah Rally of Pine Haven. She would become, if the bill passed, an Honorary Living Treasure with all attendant rights, and an annual check to cover travel and entertainment costs.

A special session of Congress was called to consider the bill to alter Sarah's status immediately. They passed it with the provision that Mrs. Rally provide receipts.

The celebrants were eating or dancing or recording events or playing whatever game the Celebration Designer suggested when Lionel and Sarah took off in their slither boats, unbeknownst to all except Ben, who saw them from his post outside the dance floor and, at the same time, realized the life guard wasn't on duty, or, if so, out of sight. He was starting for the ocean when Babe jumped on his back.

"Okay," said Ben. "One more time." There were more waves than earlier. It was getting rough. "Careful," he told Babe when they reached the water's edge. Babe plunged in. Looking beyond her he saw Sarah's boat capsize and Sarah fall into the water. *Uh oh. What was that on top of her?*

"Hang on, Babe," Ben shouted, scooping her up with his nose onto his back. At the same time, he signaled the other robots and Medivan, went into high gear and swooped to the side of Lionel's boat.

"Senator! Catch!" he called, bumping up his back in such a way that with a sharp upward movement to the right he bucked Babe toward Lionel. "I'm going for Sarah. She's in the water and there's something that shouldn't be near her—near her."

Lionel caught the soggy little dog. "Oh shit," he said.

Later Ben would wonder why Lionel hadn't gone for her himself though at the time he couldn't think of anything but rescuing Sarah. He stopped at her boat, took a dive under and around it. No Sarah—and in the distance all he saw was a blue fin gliding away.

Ben shouted to Lionel. "A tiger shark's got Sarah!"

"That's ridiculous," Lionel shouted back. "Wait."

Ben had never moved so fast before. He could see the blue-striped dorsal fin clearly but there didn't seem to be, thank God, any blood in the water so perhaps the shark had Sarah by a piece of her swimsuit. He dived down beside the shark, saw Sarah's legs thrashing below it, backed up, took aim and whopped the shark's head. The shark faltered, slumped, moved away and to Ben's relief, the rest of Sarah appeared. Together they watched the shark swim off and sink out of sight.

"Oh Ben," Sarah said, hanging on to him, dazed.

"You don't need to thank me," Ben said. "Just doing my job."

"My God mother," Clarissa said, standing in front of the Medivan, two medics, a stretcher, several crocodiles, Lionel and Babe when Ben and Sarah arrived on shore. "What on earth happened?"

"A young tiger shark snatched her," Ben said. "I saw his stripes. It's a wonder your mother's alive."

"I'm all right but I wouldn't mind lying down for a while," Sarah said, settling slowly onto the stretcher, her hand to her head.

Lionel bent over her and she whispered in his ear. "When Ben rammed the fish, I guess he rammed me, too. Just a little."

"Thank you," Clarissa said to Ben. "You saved her life."

SUNDAY, AUGUST 20, 2073

The next day, Sarah's award, her escape from a tiger shark and Roy's incarceration were all over the wall-to-wall.

"When you told me I was a Living Treasure courtesy of Congress I thought I was hallucinating," Sarah said. She and Lionel were sitting on her terrace discussing the recent events.

"I couldn't believe it either," Lionel said. He reached over to pat Sarah's hand. "Except for a slight bump on your head, everything worked out great. If it weren't for Ben you'd have made a perfect escape."

"I know. Too bad after all your trouble."

"Are you kidding? We'd have had to figure out how to get you back here."

"I'm glad I won't have to hide out for the rest of my life."

"Right."

Sarah sewed two multi-colored squares together with tiny stitches. "I wonder what's going to happen to him."

"Who?" Lionel asked.

"Roy."

"Ahh." Lionel leaned back. "Hmm. Hard to figure," he said. "The jury can't acquit Roy, even if it wants to." He closed his eyes, put his fingers together and grimaced. "So, he'll get ten years and with time off for good behavior, he'll be back in three and then he'll be living like a king off his snoop-ops."

"But he murdered Tessa."

"We'll have to wait and see, but you asked me what I thought, and that's what I think."

"If it hadn't been for you," Sarah said, "Krantz would never have arrested him. Never even known there was evidence against him."

Lionel beamed.

"You put it all together," Sarah said.

"I had quite a lot of help," Lionel said.

"But you were the force behind all the others."

"I just had a hunch."

"It still counts," Sarah said.

"But it was fun. It doesn't seem right to get credit for something I enjoyed that much."

Just then, Ben hurried by. "Take care," he said to Lionel and Sarah. "Heavy seas. Hurricane Luke is heading east away from us into the ocean so it should miss our area entirely. One earlier model had it turning west toward our island but that can't be correct because now winds are diminishing. Nevertheless, advisory to aircraft is to remain cautious. And," He looked into Sarah's aqua eyes, "absolutely no swimming."

"Don't worry," Sarah said, "Yesterday was an accident. I'm staying dry from here on."

"I just realized something," Lionel said as Ben moved on. He stroked Babe's back, kissed the bridge of her nose, turned her over and rubbed her tummy.

Sarah looked up from her quilting.

"I never took Babe for that test ride in my plane," he said.

"What about the weather?"

"We'll be fine," Lionel said. "I can bring that sweetheart down on a seashell."

"Okay," Sarah said. "I'll watch."

"Come with us."

"You're sure there's enough room?"

"It'll be a bit tight. I've gained some weight," Lionel said, "But so what? It'll be cozy."

Sarah put down her squares, stuck her needle into her red pincushion and stood. She stretched her arms over and behind her head, stooped down and picked up Babe from Lionel's lap.

"Guess what? I gave half my security diamonds to Melody and half to Zack."

"Good idea," Lionel said. "Very good." He nodded, thinking it over. "When?"

"Yesterday, before my escape." She sighed. "Attempted escape," she amended.

"Nice. Were they happy?"

"Surprised," Sarah said. "Maybe they're happy today. It takes a while for a godsend to sink in."

Zack knew it wasn't the right time, but maybe in a month or so it would be and then he'd omniplus Annemarie. Yes. By then he'd know if she was the one to go after, wouldn't he? Sure he would. She had come on so strong to him at first; he hadn't known how to handle her. He would now. He had more confidence and he had more money—or would when he sold Sarah's diamonds.

Maybe if he waited a while, Annemarie would omniplus him. That would be ideal. He hoped she wasn't talented or ambitious like Melody. He knew now Melody would never have been satisfied with a life in the mountains with children and animals to care for, but then Annemarie might not go for that either.

Maybe he was dreaming to think any woman wanted such a future—hikes, picnics, swims in the lake, watching the stars and planets—simple pleasures. To Zack, it sounded idyllic. The Dakotas were a down-to-earth people, and thus even when he was up in the air,

Zack was firmly planted. He wondered if his Indian ancestry played a part in the love he had for the land, the forests, the animals, growing and creating things out of wood—being part of nature. It didn't matter. That's the way he was, though nobody knew it, because he'd never told anyone.

"Oh no! The latest report says the storm has turned and is approaching from the east," Ben said aloud to nobody, his voice lost even to himself in the wind as he navigated as fast as he could to the airstrip where minutes before he had seen Sarah, Lionel and Babe headed. The silver duoplane was taxiing toward take-off. He had to do something drastic before it started moving faster. Lionel and Sarah saw him and were waving. Ben ran toward the plane and stopped twenty-five feet in front of its nose. It wouldn't matter if they ran him down; he could be put back together.

"Holy shit!" Lionel shouted and made a sharp right. The plane tipped over and crashed, wing down, into the river.

Ben omniplussed for the Medivan while he made a bridge of himself from land to the broken window of the cockpit. He heard barking.

"Babe," he cried. "Babe." The little dog jumped out and onto Ben's back—a clean arc. Ben could see Sarah and Lionel slumped over side by side. Neither moaned nor moved.

The Medivan arrived.

"Please," Ben said to his friends before he slid out of the way, "don't be dead."

MONDAY, AUGUST 21, 2073

Pine Haven would recover. Reaching land two hours after the airplane crash, the hurricane would have destroyed the island, but inhibited by macro-pillows and macro-projectiles, which absorbed and repelled the wind, it only uprooted a few trees. Then it blasted the peninsula protecting Swyannah, so the treasured old city escaped severe damage. Neither area had installed a sophisticated defense such as Pine Haven's.

There was just enough notice for the residents, staff and the seven crocodile sentries of Pine Haven to take refuge in the huge reinforced storm cellar beneath the hospital. It only lasted a few hours. Meanwhile, everyone was comfortable and stayed well-informed through their omnipluses and wall-to-wall. The accident made more news than the storm. The headlines told the story:

HEROINE/LIVING TREASURE FIGHTS FOR LIFE
BEN AND BABE KEEP VIGIL
ROBOT THREATENS TO KILL HIMSELF IF SARAH DIES
HEAVEN SAYS NOTHING DOING HE'S THEIR PROPERTY
BEN'S LAWYER SAYS HE BELONGS TO HIMSELF

Lionel rested in a wheelchair, his broken right arm in a HealFast cast, surveying Sarah, who lay on a hospital bed unconscious, despite a new heart, which replaced the previous one of only six years. The new one was retrieved from the hospital cold locker where all the clones of her innards and those of the other residents were labeled, freeze-dried and stored. Hydration was instantaneous and the heart inserted into her chest and connected with dispatch.

"She'll come around," one of the doctors said to Lionel, who was sitting by her side, shoulders slumped, face grim.

"She'd better," Lionel said.

I will, thought Sarah, who could hear every word. *This isn't my time to go. I'd know if it were. I'd see lights or my mother. I'd hear singing or music. I'd see my life sliding left to right before me, or scenes attached to one another like squares of my quilt falling out of sight. Also, I'm not ready. I need to forgive people across the board—even Jeff. I need to say goodbye to my children. And I'd like to tell Melody my life was worthwhile, even though I didn't do anything to write home about—I can't take credit for becoming an Honorary Living Treasure—but I'm glad for the whole confusing excursion, the accident of my life. I thank God for it all, though what He/She had in mind for any of us is still a mystery, and that's what's so exciting about what lies ahead: Answers. Lionel thinks there's just darkness and silence same as Jeff.*

"Sarah," Lionel said. "Sarah, I'm so sorry." He took her hand. It was cool. "I should have listened to Ben. It wasn't a good day for flying. I guess I was showing off."

"Again?" Sarah asked in a whispery voice.

"You're awake," Lionel said laughing at the dig. "What a relief. How do you feel?"

"Not good," she said. "What about you?" Her eyes were still closed.

"A slight concussion and a broken arm are all. No big deal." He sighed. "When you're all better, we'll go to the mountains or wherever you want."

"Sounds wonderful," Sarah said. "I'll be up and around in no time."

"Great," Lionel said. "We've a lot to celebrate."

"Like what?" Sarah asked.

"You being okay, for one, and for another, you becoming a Living Treasure."

"I don't mind dying, you know, when it's my time," Sarah said, her voice a little stronger. "I just don't want to be put down."

"I hear you," said Lionel.

"Where's Melody?" Sarah asked. "I've something I want to tell her." She opened her eyes.

"No problem," Lionel said. "She's right outside. Boy, is she going to be happy to see you. Meanwhile, I'm going down to tell Ben you're on the mend."

He stopped at the door. "Say, I don't know what this means but Zack says to tell you he'll do it."

"Tell him thanks."

"He says it wasn't because of the diamonds."

Sarah smiled. "Doesn't matter," she said.

When Lionel returned, the doctor was in Sarah's room, Melody outside looking worried.

"All of a sudden," Melody told Lionel, "Sarah stopped talking. She was in the middle of a sentence. I was holding her hand and right then, it went sort of limp."

"What was she saying?" Lionel asked.

"What a good life she'd had. Then she said it wasn't that she minded dying, but she didn't like the idea of being put down."

"Right, she told me that, too," Lionel said.

"And that it wasn't important to be important. Maybe she wanted to prepare me in case I don't make it as a singer-songwriter. Then I think she was about to tell me what *was* important when she stopped."

The doctor came out. "Sorry, Senator," he said. "Not sure what went wrong. She had a good twenty years left in her—easy." He waited for Lionel to speak, but he didn't. "We did our best, Senator."

Melody sank to the floor. "Oh, please God, no," she said.

Sarah was surprised. *Wait a minute, what's going on? Is that a light? I think so. My legs are turning to stone. Oh my God, it looks like I'm on my way—ready or not.*

The doctor patted Lionel on his cast. "The virtual autopsy will be available in a few minutes," he said.

Lionel stared at the doctor. "Is that supposed to be comforting?" he asked. "Who the hell cares? It won't bring her back."

"I'll tell Ben," Melody said through tears then sobs.

Lionel, wet-eyed, helped her up.

Tears were rare in HEAVEN. The doctor stared—a look of astonishment on his face.

Ben was horrified, distraught. "This is the worst day of my life," he said.

"It was an accident. No one blames you," Melody said.

"Wrong. I do," Ben said.

Swyannah swelled with tourists—many more than had visited at any one time before. They bought postcards of Roy and Tessa together and Roy and Tessa apart. They drank Boathouse Murderers—tomato juice, lime and gin with swizzles of imitation rocks—one on top of the other. They ate Poor Tessa Clam Rolls and Roy-Smashed Beanburgers. Mrs. Burch received all comers in her mobile home. Signs pointed the way from the jailhouse:

CONTRIBUTE TO ROY'S DEFENSE
AND MEET HIS SWEET MAMA

To repay people for the trouble they took in walking a mile to the field, and their generous contributions to Roy's defense once there, the twins served them homemade iced lemony tea and divine sugar pecan cookies, both, they said, family recipes from the late eighteen hundreds. Their hospitality became so well-known—they were shown wall-to-wall, smiling ear-to-ear, day and night—that even more thrill-seekers arrived, many camping out, for a fee, on Mrs. Burch's field; the town's accommodations were full and reserved for weeks to come. Mrs. Burch and the twins were suddenly almost as famous as Roy.

SATURDAY, AUGUST 26, 2073

Ben began the funeral service on the beach for Sarah, the no-longer-Living Treasure, who lay perfectly preserved, courtesy of HEAVEN, for all to view, inside a see-through blue nylocks casket, impervious to the elements, angled at a gentle twenty-five degrees on a platform in front of the dais and lectern. Zack brought the eleva-wheel over from the StrataDrome via the aerohearse. Ben scooted onto it and Zack raised the device so that Ben's head was, for once, higher than everyone's. He looked down at the huge assembly, which had gathered by boat or plane because of the publicity attending Sarah's death and her recent fame. HEAVEN'S HEROINE DIES was in headlines all over the wall-to-wall and the two national papers.

"I wanted to save their lives and, instead, Sarah is dead and it's my fault," Ben said. "I'll never forgive myself. She was a terrific person. She loved people, animals, and me, and she remained true to her principles and didn't rat on anyone—not even Tessa, who tried to drown her. Melody has written a song in her honor. Here she is with the CrossOvers.

Huxley strummed a few bars. "Ladies and gentlemen, please welcome Miss Melody Graves singing Heaven is Blue."

"Missing you," Melody sang.
"Heaven is blue,
So SO blue.
'Cause we're miss miss missing you,

Here in Heaven,
Heaven is blue…"

"You know what, Miss Melody, honey?" Huxley asked after she sang it through again and the applause was nearly over,. "That was beautiful. I've said it before and I'll say it again—you've got a future."

Ben wondered what kind of future Huxley actually foresaw for her. Melody had a lovely voice but the song she wrote was, at best, ordinary—trite music and empty lyrics. Huxley must know that. What was going on? He watched them stare at each other, faces aglow.

Ben was worried. Not understanding the man-woman thing meant his dissertation would suffer. On the other hand, Zack had promised to let him interview him, and Lionel said he could listen to his autobiographical recordings. That should help. Then, if Melody would tell him what she knows about Sarah's life, and what she'd be willing to tell him about her own, maybe Homo sapiens would start to make some kind of sense.

Lionel spoke next. He said he'd been bad luck to the important women in his life, including Sarah. He told the assembly the accident was his fault, not Ben's. He should have been in control of his plane, no matter what, and he shouldn't have been flying to begin with—even before the hurricane turned. There was too much wind. He told them he'd asked Sarah to marry him though not that she was asleep at the time, that she was his good friend, and so he was taking her to his mountain home where a piece of his property was grandfathered for legal burials. She'd be interred near where he'd rest when his time came, and where his son and wives lay waiting. Sarah's family had given him permission, and he wanted to thank them publicly.

If he hadn't proposed to Sarah, he thought later, *she wouldn't have been jinxed—would probably still be alive. On the other hand she hadn't heard him.*

Well, damn it all to hell, he couldn't help her now—so that had to be that, and for the rest of his days, he'd have to be satisfied with the pleasure of Babe's company and trying to write mysteries, which was a lot harder than he'd thought. He had begun an outline and it seemed familiar, sort of like *The Maltese Falcon*, his favorite mystery, but not as complex. Solving them was easier and more fun, but it wasn't every day there was a murder under his nose.

MONDAY, AUGUST 28, 2073

Harriet was tired, exhausted from the excitement of the past several days even though she only knew the people involved through Melody: There was Tessa's death and memorial service; Roy's confession, imprisonment and impending trial; Sarah's rescue from a tiger-shark; Sarah and Lionel's crash; the hurricane; Sarah's death and funeral. This wasn't her idea of a blissful life. Now Huxley was on his way to discuss future plans. Something was up. It almost sounded as if he'd changed his mind about moving to the southwest. She dragged herself outdoors to lie on her chaise, read *The Road to Selfdom*, written by one of her former colleagues, and wait for Huxley.

"A pretty nice day all in all," Ben declared to each person or open door he cruised by in his area of responsibility, one-seventh of Pine Haven Island. "A bit on the warm side. Temperature eighty-six degrees, skies cloudy, ocean calm. No wind." Ben, robot extraordinaire, and first among six other robot crocodiles, paused at Harriet's terrace.

"Hi Ben. Do you know the time?" she asked.

"Ten after five," he answered.

"You didn't by any chance see Huxley, did you?" she asked.

"I believe he's headed this way." Ben paused. "With a friend," he added.

"Really?" Harriet sat up. "Who?"

"See for yourself," Ben said, and there was Huxley, strolling toward them, still at a distance, Melody beside him. They were holding hands.

Harriet jumped up and hugged herself. "Oh my God—it's Melody. No one will believe this—my son and that lovely girl, my Angelic, who sings like an angel." She flung her arms out. "How perfect. I love it. Love it!"

Then as Ben watched in amazement and dismay, she did two cramp rolls, four time steps and several circular shuffle ball changes while humming tunelessly in accompaniment.

"I think there's going to be a happy ending," she warbled and pivoted toward Ben. "Don't you?"

No, Ben would have liked to say. *Sarah gone forever—Lionel and Babe set to fly around the country looking for unsolved murders with leads—Zack uncommunicative, mooning over Annemarie—and now Melody, about to go off with Huxley who, the whole island and Swyannah knew, was moving southwest. Harriet probably would point out that what she just said was only a manner of speaking, because she's got to know there are no happy endings—only happy beginnings—which is why starting over is so popular. On the other hand, humans are expert at ignoring the obvious. I'll put that in my dissertation.*

Harriet executed four quick flaps and cakewalked toward him. "Don't you?" she beseeched.

Ben sighed. It was pointless to tell her what he thought. A waste of breath, so to speak, and besides—anything was possible

"Absolutely," he said. "No question."